D1342357

Jenni Hutchinson is a Christian socialist Arsenal fan from Chandlers Ford in Hampshire. She is currently living in Bradford and training to be a Citizenship teacher. *Just my Job* was written during a stint volunteering in Malawi with Ripple Africa.

Dedication

Thanks to God for my life and talent, my family, friends and football for supporting and inspiring me, and Malawi for giving me the space and time to finally finish a book.

Jenni Hutchinson

Just My Job

A CIP catalogue record for this title is available from the British Library.

ISBN 978 184963 369 7

www.austinmacauley.com

First Published (2014)
Austin Macauley Publishers Ltd.
25 Canada Square
Canary Wharf
London
E14 5LB

Printed and bound in Great Britain

Prologue

"Your mother gave you a name today, although she doesn't realise it," Great Father says to me, not long after I've finished my breakfast.

"How can she do it without realising it?" I ask. There are a lot of things I don't yet understand.

"It was related to something her friend Mr Barkley said. He planted the idea of giving this name to a child in her head, but I know she will never do it. She loves this name, and she loves you, so it is yours."

Great Father tells me the name. It's smooth, with a wave in it, like the sea, and reminds me of music. At once, I feel new life in me, because he has called me by name. He had told me that this would happen. Before now, everybody called me sweet names that weren't only mine – darling, dear, pumpkin and my favourite, *kochanie*. It's my favourite because it makes the best sound.

"Now, what shall we play?" he asks.

"Can we play any game in the world?"

"Of course. You know that."

"Can we play chess?" I ask.

Great Father looks surprised, but is still smiling.

"The last time we played chess, you gave up, and told me that it was too old for you."

"Pradziadek taught me."

Pradziadek was the first family member that I met, and he looks like an old man. Great Father says that he doesn't ever want me to look like an old woman. He says that when my mother arrives, she'll look about twenty two, and that it will be nice if I look around fourteen then, so that she can see me grow. After that, I can also stop at twenty two eventually.

Pradziadek doesn't speak English, but he sat me down and worked out a chess game on his own, and I watched and learned. Pradziadek didn't always live here. Like most people here, he had a different kind of life somewhere else once, which I didn't. I don't yet know why. The easiest way to explain it is that I woke up here, in my own bed, but didn't remember going to bed – either here, or anywhere else. Great Father was by my side when I awoke. He gave me breakfast, and then we played Ludo, because he said I was English, and that English children seemed to learn the colours red, blue, yellow and green before all the others.

Then he started reading books with me. From the picture books that he showed me at first, I know that I look about five years old right now. Great Father told me that I haven't been here as long as five years, but that bringing years into the world we know was a difficult thing to do. He tried to explain to me how a year worked, but it made my brain go funny, and he said that when people in other places try and imagine how our time works, that makes their brains go funny, too.

Soon I learned to read. I learned about mothers and fathers. He told me that I had one of each, but that they would have to join me later. I sort of know that what happens to me here with Great Father is important *now*, and that what my mother and father are doing elsewhere is what the grown-ups here call 'a distraction'. I still like to ask about them, though, and Great Father doesn't mind.

"Will Mr Barkley join us one day too?" I ask Great Father as he sets up the chessboard.

"Yes. Why do you keep asking me if people will come? You know they will."

He looks over at his stack of books. The book he wrote is the most important of all, with its list of co-authors – as long as my wavy, messy, blonde hair – embossed on the front in gold. It always sits on top of the pile, but today, he selects another.

"You're a little young for *Revelations of Divine Love*, aren't you? I'll give it to you…" He looks at me, and puts it away again. "I'll give it to you just before your mother comes. You will be able to teach her about it. She has some very *uninspired* views," he says, in the same voice that he uses when I make a mistake – full of love and care.

I move my pawn to D4, and Great Father chuckles.

"Pradziadek is good at this, isn't he?" he says, stroking his famous beard.

1

Hi, I'm Kate.

Oh, don't worry. You don't need to know about me for a long time. In fact, depending on whether you're experiencing this before or after the 12th May 2015, I may not even have been born yet. How am I telling you this? No idea really, but I believe it has something to do with God. You may have other ideas.

All I know is that at my fortieth birthday party, my mum got a little drunk and started telling all these wonderful old stories. At the end of a particularly emotive and important one, we were all wide-eyed with astonishment.

"You have to make that story known, Mum," I said, still trying to drag myself back into the present. "It's like the greatest story ever told or something."

"Do you think so?" she faltered, ever amazed to hear that she was capable of the extraordinary, in spite of the sixty four years of extraordinary life she has lived so far. "Well, if anyone writes it down, it should be you, Kate. You're the one who's good with stories."

I started off writing stories for my kids – Naomi, Louise and Adam – before setting up a website dedicated to creating literacy resources for primary schools.

My granddad started to make all these conservative noises about how somebody could get hurt.

"I'm writing down Mum's story, Gramp, not felling giant Redwoods," I retorted, but we all love him, and are happy that he can still make coherent noises at ninety. Anyway, I went away and spent the next six weeks writing it all down, but changed all the names, so that nobody could get hurt.

However, one night when I unusually couldn't sleep, I got this sense that there were people who could learn the full details without anyone getting hurt. That if I just sat in my dark room and talked into the night, somebody would hear, and the greatest story ever told would reach a generation that might otherwise never hear it. That somebody there might love it as much as I do, and decide that this story should never be lost… I felt like I *should* do it, because it would cause me no harm and cause others great good, but there was no pain in the obligation. The last time I had felt like this was when I was sixteen and gave my life to Jesus. It was easy, and I knew, straightaway, that God had come into my life and would not let me go, so I wanted to serve Him. Until now, everything I've felt like I ought to do for God has been met with stubbornness and frustration inside me. Now, comfortable in the natural knowledge that what I am about to do is right before God, I wonder if everything else I was feeling had anything to do with him at all, but I push this thought aside for later, because I have a story to tell.

And so, we begin. Meet Lily McGoldrick. She comes from Ryde on the Isle of Wight, and goes to Southampton University, right across the water. She reads surprisingly little for an English Literature major, and wishes she had taken something else. She fills her time with friends, sports, drinking and student activism – socialising and socialism. She is smart enough to do this, and also to pass her course – and pass it well.

The government's constant variation of fees, grants and loans mean that this year, Lily has decided to sacrifice some of her social life in order to be able to eat enough to live. Previously, she relied on seasonal work at home for extra income, but most of that was swallowed up by her summer holiday. We therefore meet Lily McGoldrick as she trudges into Hope Stores on a Monday morning. She is joining the ever-increasing brigade of students who work part-time during term time.

Hope Stores is a local, family-run cash and carry that has been catapulted into unexpected greatness by the recession. Lily wonders if it is called Hope because Quakers or an equally hopeful religious organisation founded it, but actually, one Norman Hope was responsible. His son David now runs the business, but the person Lily needs to speak to is the personnel manager, Sue Hill.

"Morning," Lily says to the rotund security guard she encounters as soon as she enters. "It's my first day, and I need to see Sue Hill."

'Insecure Jim' is the cruel nickname of Jim Trollope, the security man. The employee who named him thus had little faith in the large, middle-aged Jim's ability to apprehend thieves. In actual fact, he is surprisingly fast over short distances, and when was the last time anyone saw a guard pursue an offender beyond about four rows of the store car park? Jim also happens to be emotionally insecure; he is forever fretting over what his wife Veronica sees in him, and is troubled by her sexual and racial stereotyping of his deputy, Frank Nwachukwu. He is also very, very good at his job. It is astonishing what an eye with twenty years of experience can see that the most athletic bouncer's eye misses.

"Yes, Sue's upstairs," says Jim, shifting in his seat to hand Lily a visitor's pass. "First on the right. Hope it goes well for you today, love."

Sue turns out to be a small, smiley and elegant woman in her mid-thirties. She joined the staff of Hope's, where her mother worked, aged sixteen, and has never regretted her decision – it was that or an office job with the local undertaker, which didn't really float her boat.

"Nice to meet you, Lily. We were expecting you yesterday, but I see you're not down to work Sundays, so that can't be right, can it?" She shakes her head at the inaccurate rota before her. "People don't think before they type around this place. I'm just as guilty, but then the reason I work in a place like Hope's is because I can't spell, so why do they give me all the sign writing to do?"

Sue was one of the many victims of undiagnosed dyslexia at school; she still doesn't know that this is behind her literacy problems.

Sue chatters away as she finds Lily a size 10 shirt, long length trousers and an accurate name badge – "It was a close run thing, you were nearly Bob" – before concluding, "Right, so, if you just clock in like this, I'll take you to meet Jacek, and he can show you the ropes."

Jacek is stacking biscuits with his aquiline side profile to Lily as she approaches. He is working in a silent, determined manner that is imperious and thoroughly masculine. He is fair, and although he has neither killer cheekbones nor a slightly receding hairline, it wouldn't be any more obvious that he was Polish if he was playing in goal and drinking 75% proof vodka at the same time. What Jacek doesn't know is that the characteristics he is displaying at this moment in time, limited though they are, are beginning to do things to Lily's pulse rate.

"Jacek, this is our new little star, Lily."

He turns to greet Sue and takes in Lily; five foot six, slim, small but firm bosoms, unusually long legs. Her straightened and layered brown hair falls to just below her shoulders. Her eyes are pixie green. Jacek breaks into his natural, welcoming smile.

It is finished.

"Good morning." A deep, gravelly voice with a strong enough Polish accent to give our Lily deep shocks, yet with the clear confidence of a good English speaker, and a hint of question intonation that betrays that Jacek is cheeky.

Lily gathers all her courage, thanks the Lord in heaven for her old flatmate Kasia, smiles back, offers her hand and shyly says, "Dzien dobry."

Jacek leans back in surprise, takes her hand, and says, "Lily, that was brilliant."

A friendship that will endure several thousand uninteresting hours of work – and an awful lot else – has been cemented. But Jacek and Lily don't know about the awful lot else yet.

2

"So, how's your first day going?" asks Sue, when she and Lily catch up in the staff canteen four hours later.

"Fine, thanks," says Lily breezily. "I was hoping to go on the checkouts, and thought shelf stacking would be really boring, but it's fine."

It would be a bit boring if Lily had to stack shelves on her own. The Hope's management have realised this, and usually ask colleagues to work in twos or threes. Lily is getting used to some of the quirkier requirements of the job – things that she never would have expected to have to do. For example, if a customer asks her where something is, she has to take them to the product, even if it's at the other end of the store. If anybody thanks her for her efforts, she is supposed to say, "No problem – it's just my job," although different words with similar sentiment are tolerated. The phrase has become something of a joke at Hope's. People say it when they are thanked for holding the cloakroom door open, for example, and Jacek has an amusing way of making the phrase as dark as an epitaph when he really doesn't want to do something.

"It's fine, or Jacek's fine? Don't worry," Sue interjects as she sees Lily blush. "We all think he's a dish – well, it's not really arguable, is it? You really impressed him with that bit of Polish, I can tell."

"My room-mate at uni taught it to me," explains Lily. "He did seem very pleased."

She has a question that she really ought to ask Sue, but something stops her. She needs to find out, at some stage, whether the game she plans to play is futile. However, now is not the time. She wants that period of wondering, dreaming, scheming. She's quite prepared to be brought down to earth eventually, but Jacek hasn't said anything about "my wife" yet.

Lily isn't working with Jacek in the afternoon – he has supervisory stuff to do – but she meets two friendly coworkers named Janet and Lynn. Janet is middle-class, and married to an ageing PE teacher who she's trying to convince to switch to his second subject – Physics – before the next torn ligament. Lynn, five years younger, is a single mother of three grown-up children and looking forward to spending her middle years doing all the things she never got to do as a young woman, because she fell pregnant at seventeen. Janet and Lynn each have a child at Southampton University, although Lily doesn't know either of them, probably because they take such alien subjects (Mathematics and Engineering). Lily is very pleased to discover that Lynn's engineer is a girl, as the faculty has traditionally been male-dominated. Both women find Lily to be polite, funny and a fast learner – a perfect new colleague. Lily would never consider the idea that she is perfect – well, not seriously. Only in the way that everyone does – that innate sense of righteousness that few can claim to have truly defeated. Lily is confident, not arrogant, and tries to be honest; she is aware of some of her flaws. None of those that she knows about would be immediately apparent to a pair of middle-aged women, since Lily is twenty and heterosexual, and every self-inflicted problem she has ever had has been grounded in unrequited love.

That night, Lily performs a verbal post-mortem of her first day with flatmate Coral.

"A man?" asks Coral straightaway when Lily returns from work, singing, and brighter than usual in the face.

"You've no idea," breathes Lily. "*The* man. Jacek Bogdanowski. This is the one. I can feel it."

"Yeah, but how many times have you said that?"

"Every time. That's what you do. You give it a few weeks, or a month, and if you don't feel that innate safety and confidence, the knowledge that you could spend the rest of your life with this guy and it would be okay, then it's time to end the relationship."

"Yeah, but they always dump you. When have you ever ended a relationship?"

"Not always. I dumped Arthur."

"Quite right, too. He was a dick."

"Not always..."

Coral prevents a circular discussion. "So, describe this Jacek Bogdanowski, then."

"About six feet tall, blond, late twenties, not particularly remarkable in looks alone, but he's got this *thing* about him. He's charismatic. He has the hottest Polish accent I've ever heard, and his smile would melt the polar ice caps. And he's really funny and nice."

"Sounds promising," says Coral.

* * *

"Ugh," says Tonia later. "I don't think I could fancy a Polish guy."

"Yeah, but if you got to know him..."

"I bet he would say he couldn't fancy a black girl," says Tonia, who is half Ghanaian and half Malawian.

"Not necessarily, although a lot of people seem to say that," admits Lily.

"Most of the Poles I've met are racist," interjects Heidi.

The four Literature students are at their favourite table in the local student pub, the Stile, drinking San Miguel as it's the beginning of term and they are feeling flush. They will be on strict rations of one Carling a week by December.

"They'll tell you they're not, but my Polish ex-boyfriend called the Cameroon football team 'monkeys', tried to pretend he was joking, and seemed embarrassed whenever we ended up in the same room as somebody black or Asian."

"It's more socially acceptable to be racist over there than over here," says Lily, who went to Poland to visit Kasia the previous summer and tried her best to engage with the culture. "It's because there are hardly any black or Asian people over there, and all attempts to prevent racism come from the Government down, not from ordinary people. So young people rebel against it by using all these stupid racist words, and if you try and tell politicians that social attitudes can only change if ordinary people accept that the status quo is wrong, they'll call you an anarchist or Communist."

"Which you are," says Coral.

"Irrelevant! Social change from the bottom up works. It's empirically proven. Look at the near-eradication of racist chanting from English football stadiums..."

"No, I don't want to," teases Tonia. "Assuming your new man won't be embarrassed to be in the same room as me, when do we get to meet him?"

3

As Lily gets to know Jacek, she increasingly likes what she sees. Tonia most certainly has nothing to fear from a man whose social intercourse is so fluid and easy. The only person Jacek seems to have an irrational problem with is Jim.

"Jim and I are going to watch the football later on, Jacek. Do you want to come?" invites Lily, a week or so after her first day at Hope's.

Lily supports Arsenal, and they are opening their 2011-12 Champions League campaign that night, against Borussia Dortmund.

"Jim?" says Jacek incredulously. "Why do you want to drink with him?"

"He's my friend," says Lily, confused.

"As long as you are only friends."

"He's married. Anyway, what if I did have a thing for older men? Jim's friendly and funny. I could do a lot worse."

Jacek draws Jim's corpulent figure with his hands. "You deserve someone more handsome."

It is Jacek's first indication that he is possessed of flaws; also, the first sign that he finds Lily attractive.

*　　*　　*

"So stay slim, Tonia, and you'll be fine in his eyes," Lily giggles that night in the bar.

Jim hasn't arrived yet, and Lily needs to get the Jacek obsessing out of the way before another Hope's colleague is present.

"You still think he's wonderful?" asks Coral, pushing away her chips. Coral is a size 12 to 14 and perfectly proportioned, but weight talk always says 'diet time' to her.

"He's an idiot sometimes, but nobody's perfect, and he's still perfect to me. We just click. Sparks fly when we're together."

"You can't deny the facts of liiiiiife…" sings Heidi, and everybody laughs.

The girls turn their attention to the TV, where Arsenal and their German opponents have just taken to the field.

"Do you know what I'm going to do?" says Lily, suddenly and excitedly. "I'm going to find out what football team Jacek supporters, and get Kasia to send me their shirt or something. I don't have a Polish team yet."

"Or you could support their deadly rivals – that might make it more fun," observes Heidi.

"You know what would suck?" asks Coral. "If he doesn't support Polish football at all and prefers Spurs or Chelsea."

"That would be weird," giggles Tonia. "That would be like me supporting Dinamo Zagreb or something."

"They say that in Russia, supporting your local first division team can be as remote as living in London and supporting Sparta Prague," observes Lily; and then the match starts, and the women temporarily shut up.

* * *

"Man United are short sighted, tra la la la la la la la la," sings Lily. She has just seen Jacek's keyring. It seems Coral was right!

"Behave. Who do you support?"

"Arsenal, Arsenal, Arsenal…" sings Lily.

"What? What happened the weekend before last?"

"An aberration!" says Lily dramatically, flinging out her arms. "A horrible thing that happens once every ten years. My brother and I theorised that it was part of the Illuminati conspiracy or something. That Alex Ferguson heads along to that owl-burning ritual in America once a decade to wreak havoc on us."

The previous Sunday, Manchester United had beaten Arsenal by 8 goals to 2. It had been 6-1 in 2001 and 6-2 in the late '80s or early '90s – Lily can never quite remember, and since she possibly wasn't born, nobody can really blame her.

"What-burning?"

"Owl. Bird that flies at night and goes 'twit-twoo'. Delivers Harry Potter's mail and can spell his own name W-O-L."

"I have never read any Harry Potter book or seen any film."

Probably the most intelligent available response to the last minute's conversation. Did I mention that Lily is odd? Delightfully so, in many opinions – including Jacek's – but undeniably so.

The day continues fairly normally. Lily finds out that Jacek's relatives have lived in Essex since the Second World War.

"So they bought you a Man U shirt, obviously," quips Lily.

No, he and his parents came to visit them for a whole month in 1999 and Man United won the treble while they were there. Jacek was fifteen.

"Lucky you – it's not your first football memory," says Lily dolefully. "I started supporting Arsenal when we lost the FA Cup semi-final to you guys. Just missed two trophies, and had to wait three years for another two."

She simultaneously loves and despises that Jacek finds this hilarious – another spark in their incendiary friendship.

Suddenly, all is quiet. A booming female voice can be heard over the gentle babble of colleague banter and Wave 105, the varied yet inoffensive local radio station.

"This shelf should have been full and free of rubbish by 8am, Lydia. It's 9.30. Why are there still cardboard boxes everywhere?"

Lydia, an eighteen-year-old grocery colleague, hangs her head, and doubles the speed of her work. The booming voice belongs to Sally Hill, Sue's very different older sister. Sally did very well at school, went to university, and got a good job at an insurance firm; then, two years later, came home and started being nasty to everybody. Nobody has ever got to the bottom of Sally's abrupt career and personality change. She has never married. She and her sister still share the same name because Sue married someone called Derek Hill, which was handy in a no-new-chequebook kind of way.

Sally's reign of terror is due to last all day, Jacek and Lily note dispiritedly, and Lily feels both relieved and guilty when she leaves for class at noon, leaving Jacek to put up with it alone.

The next day, Lily has another 8am to 12 noon shift. She hasn't had much sleep, having prioritised a fantasy about giving Jacek a long massage to soothe away the stress of having to work with horrible managers. She loves how such fantasies make her feel; so much better than the purely sexual ones. The pleasure seems to be centred on mid-oesophagus, shortening the breath and complementing Jacek-induced knots in the stomach. The sensation is both relaxing and stimulating – kind of like the experience she was dreaming about would be – and Lily slept incredibly well once the daydream had run its course. It's just that this didn't happen until at about one o' clock in the morning.

Lily has been having issues with her phone since she set the default language to Polish, with the intent to learn some. Jacek never saw her phone before she did it – or, for that matter, since she did it – so he incorrectly assumes she's had it like this for longer than the last two weeks.

"It's doing odd, Anglicised things," Lily says, as she opens yet another box with a Stanley knife and pulls hot chocolate sachets onto the shelf before her. "Obviously, I usually text in English, but when I text in Polish, it remembers that I'm English. It says 'sang' instead of 'Pani'. It says 'pilla' when I'm trying to write about pilka nozna, and honestly, I can't think of anything I write more often…" 'Pilka nozna' means football.

"Will you stop talking and do some work, please?" barks Sally from the end of the aisle. Lily is sensitive to criticism, and hypersensitive to unjust criticism, but old enough not to shout back, or burst into tears. However, she cannot let unfair accusations go; she feels she should not, or other people could suffer the same unfairness. She has a box and a knife in her hand. It ought to be perfectly obvious that she is multi-tasking.

"I *am* talking and working at the same time, Sally," Lily said, straightforwardly and mildly.

Sally is not in a rational mood. Sally is rarely in a rational mood.

"No, you weren't! You were talking to Jacek, and it's all you ever do! And you..." she says, rounding on Jacek, "Your job as a supervisor is to stop people talking so that the work gets done. If it doesn't, you'll be staying on to finish it."

Lily is wounded – she doesn't yet know the extent of Sally's misanthropy, doesn't know that no one can work at Hope's without falling victim to it. Is she, Lily, really letting her work suffer? Is she really making more work for the person she cares about more than anyone else? She turns ashamedly away from Jacek and cuts into a box firmly, dispelling the tension through her fingers.

Jacek is appalled by Sally's behaviour. He walks up behind Lily, gently tickles her elbow and intones, "Don't worry about it," in her ear – gravelly as ever, but soft.

He then goes for an emergency cigarette, hoping to take the edge off his frustration with Sally. Not for Jacek, the sadistic pleasure of nurturing a bad mood and exploding randomly in the face of innocent parties.

A package has arrived, addressed to Jacek Bogdanowski, signed, sealed and delivered. It is Lily McGoldrick's heart, and he had better be careful what he does with it. Jacek is unaware of this new responsibility, and although every encounter with Lily seems to lighten his spirit, his emotional response to her cannot go any further. Yet.

4

Lily is nothing if not charismatic. The only person who would ever describe her as 'boring' is Tonia, and this is part teasing and part a reflection of their entirely different interests. As well as her encyclopaedic knowledge of a diverse range of subjects, Lily holds people's attention through her brightness, enthusiasm, jokes and sense of drama. She can turn an everyday irrelevance into the conversational equivalent of a Booker Prize winner. She isn't bad looking, but is no model, and it is her personality that attracts men – an increasing number of men, in fact.

The following Monday, Lily goes to work after a normal weekend. Lily and her friends obsessed about the fate of their various football teams over a Saturday pub lunch in front of Sky Sports News, then spent the evening arguing over which bar to go to. Lily won – Lily does not usually win – and her reward was a trip to Firehouse, a rock club. Coral surprised herself by having a good time, Lily and Heidi braved the mosh pit, and Tonia went home with the phone number of a much older, heavily pierced, but undeniably attractive man called Simon.

"He almost had a Jacek air about him," admits Lily on the way home. "No – don't jump down my throat! It's true!"

Lily expects a groaning chorus of requests to stop bringing Jacek into every conversation, and heads it off by quickly continuing, "They have an identical manner, similar sense of humour… I think Simon seems nicer, though. Softer round the edges."

"So Jacek isn't nice?" Tonia dares to suggest.

"Not always – but when it counts…" breathes Lily.

The girls have all heard the story of how Jacek rescued Lily's day, and her self-esteem, after Sally behaved so malevolently. They all agree that such a rescue would have made each of them go wobbly too.

Sunday always begins with church for Lily and Tonia, although they go to very different churches – Tonia's is fairly exclusively African, doesn't teach Scripture very intelligently in Lily's opinion, and the service sometimes lasts four hours. Tonia isn't stupid, or especially fundamentalist, but church has always been this way for her, and she has friends there from the African Society at university. Lily plays semi-safe: she goes to the local Anglican Church's student service. The leaders present challenging messages about how students should live their lives, and Lily doesn't always agree with their slightly simplistic teachings, but she tries to put them whatever she feels she can into practice, and sometimes, usually when sad or lonely, she feels very close to God there. After all, He was meant to whisper in pleasure and shout in pain and whatever the middle, speaking one was.

These last few weeks, Lily has been floating on air, but there is no guilt in her pleasure. She therefore finds it easy to worship God and give thanks for how good she is feeling, and get a feeling of engagement with Him from this kind of worship, too – the Oh-Lord-you're-great kind, rather than the O-Lord-the-clouds-are-gathering kind.

In the afternoon, first Lily, then Tonia, return home and drag first Coral, then Heidi, out of bed. Lily lives with Coral and Tonia lives with Heidi, at opposite ends of Portswood – a part of Southampton known to be cheap and full of students and immigrants. Perfect for Lily, the young xenophile. The girls tidy their houses and do undone work, then settle down to quiet pleasures. Lily practices Polish and Coral bakes a cake, which the pair then eat with tea in front of Antiques Roadshow, because students are permitted to geek out in front of the programmes their parents watch, without shame. Tonia goes swimming while Heidi continues to make herself a fashionable jumpsuit, a project she fears will take just enough time for them to become unfashionable. Tonia then does her best to reverse the good she has done by buying chips on the way home, and she and Heidi eat them in front of Top Gear. Sundays in Studentdom, all in all, are the perfect bliss that God intended them to be, even if you weren't meant to iron or finish assignments on them, and the pool staff shouldn't have been working.

(That is, you were neither meant to iron nor finish assignments. I'm sure nobody irons their assignments anyway, unless the cat sleeps on them. But still, I apologise. Like Lily, I was a Literature major – European, not just English – and ambiguity deserves no place in the greatest story ever told. But I digress).

So, it's Monday again, and Lily is at work at 8am. She walks into the warehouse. Jacek is standing by a computer with a very attractive woman, which doesn't bother Lily at all. There is a wonderful lack of fear or jealousy in her current infatuation: miraculously, given how these things usually turn out, it has been good for her.

"Dzien dobry, Jacek."

"Dzien dobry… Oh, Lily, I would like you to meet my girlfriend, Gabriela. She starts here today."

Punched in the stomach, in the exact same place where on Thursday she'd felt the warmth of Jacek's comfort, Lily still manages to say "Bardzo mi milo, jestem Lily." (Very nice to meet you, I'm Lily.)

She gets a good look at Gabriela, and realises she was wrong. Gabriela is not attractive. She is beautiful, stunning. She has a sheet of epically long straight white-blonde hair, and honey-coloured eyes. She is taller than Lily, with the same amount of chest and less waist. Her nails are filed and painted, and her teeth gleam white. She wears just a tiny amount of make-up, covering imperfections that aren't there in order to be seen to be using make-up, in Lily's opinion – unless she is incredibly insecure, which would be weird, considering she looks like Barbie and is going out with Jacek.

"Oh, you speak Polish," says Gabriela, smiling. "That's nice. Where did you learn?"

Lily explains about Kasia. The punched stomach is beginning to feel more like emptiness, the empty place where her dreams once lay, but the pain has not really started in earnest. A familiar feeling, later softened a little by the realisation that it could have been worse – she could have been his wife!

"Oh, that is nice," says Gabriela again, displaying the descriptive vocabulary of an infant school child, before returning to speaking full-on Polish with Jacek.

Over the next few weeks, Lily ends up working alongside Gabriela, and tries to bring her out a little. Lily tries to challenge her first impression of people, rather than reinforce it, with limited success. She seems to have been right about Gabriela,. The nineteen-year-old beauty's conversation revolves around her appearance, trying to lose weight (she is a size 6), being tired, eating chocolate, shopping. There seems to be nothing unique about Gabriela. No special interests and no personality quirks that make people want to talk to her. No sense of humour of her own – she laughs at other people's jokes, but does not make them. In short, Gabriela is nice, but boring.

What is going on here? Nice –But boring girls do not usually end up with guys like Jacek – charismatic, confident, funny and flirty. They end up with nice –But boring guys. You know the type: he spends Saturday afternoon waiting for the football scores, and Sunday either playing football or round his mum's for Sunday lunch. He works in a shop or an office, or studies Sports Science or Business Studies. He indulges in the occasional round of golf or game of darts. He buys expensive trainers, and loves his dog and his mum. He wears a Help for Heroes wristband… Come to think of it, this is Mr Nice –But Boring English style, and Lily has no idea how a similar Polish guy would behave. But still. How can Jacek live with someone who doesn't return the sparks that he generates? For live with her he does.

"Maybe he needs his sparks earthed," says Heidi wisely as the four girls dissect the situation in the pub for the umpteenth time.

"Up to a point, I agree," admits Lily, "but I know relationships like that, where he's excessive, kind of simple and a bit hedonistic, and she's reining him in in an assertive way – joking with him, telling him she doesn't love him anymore because her shift finishes two hours later, thoroughly enjoying dragging him round the shops on her birthday. Gabriela absorbs rather than earths, I'd say. I'm surprised she doesn't get electrocuted and run away or something."

"He's not a live rail," says Tonia condescendingly, but she's smiling. She's not being mean – she's just being Tonia.

"He is a livewire, and she's a damp squib. I have no idea how it works."

"So steal him," encourages Coral.

"No," sighs Lily, "that wouldn't be fair. If it really works, good luck to them both. If it doesn't – well, then I'll be waiting."

5

Waiting is what Lily does, for a rather long time, but not exclusively; she isn't one to pine away. She throws herself into uni, politics, church, friends – anything that comes along. Plus, she has a twenty-first birthday to plan. It falls on Guy Fawkes Night, which suits Lily down to the ground.

"I'd love to have an ultras-themed birthday party," she enthuses at work. "Everyone has to bring some kind of hand-held pyro – sparklers are okay, flares are better. We'll all wear our football shirts – or better, unofficial T-shirts – and scarves, preferably hand-knitted or from a supporters' club rather than anything official. If you don't have anything like that, don't worry – a plain or stripy scarf will do, or I've got loads that I can lend."

"Not in my size, you haven't," chuckles Jim. "Good job I've got a ten-year-old "Be a Gooner for a day" T-shirt – you'll like that, won't you, Lily?" Lily nods in agreement.

Jacek is not privy to this conversation. Once Lily has arranged a venue – well, agreed with Coral that the flat they share does indeed have an ideally sized garden and no known neighbourhood dogs – and a time, she invites him personally.

"Sorry, I can't make it," he says. "Too busy."

Not "It's my friend's birthday," Not "I'm already going to a firework party," Not "You suck and I'd rather hang out with a scared dog on Firework Night." Just "Too busy."

Over the next few weeks, a pattern emerges.

"Want to come to the cinema with me and the girls to see the latest Twilight episode? Gabriela's welcome too."

"Sorry, too busy."

"Want to watch the Man U game with us – that is, if you don't mind us cheering for the opposition?"

"Too busy."

"Are you and Gabriela coming to the Christmas do?"

"No, sorry, I'm far too busy."

Busy doing what? Lily wonders. He doesn't have kids, and she knows what hours he works. He spends about an hour a day on Facebook, but then, who doesn't? She doesn't think he cooks, and she's never spotted him in the Polish club or any other local hostelry.

Jacek does, indeed, like Facebook, although he strictly rations his time on the computer. He enjoys speculating about his friends through applications like '21 Questions'.

"Do you think Lily McGoldrick is a member of the Mile High Club?" – Yes.

"Do you think Lily McGoldrick has ever been skinny-dipping?" – Yes.

"Do you think Lily McGoldrick is hot?"

"What are you doing, *kochanie*?" asks Gabriela, appearing next to him from nowhere.

"Just this stupid Facebook game," says Jacek, hastily pressing 'No'. This is a lie, but Lily wouldn't take such things too seriously – would she?

* * *

'Jacek Bogdanowski has answered a question about you!' says an email in Lily's inbox. 'To find out what Jacek said, log on to Facebook.'

Lily is excited. All she has had so far from this application is old school friends saying 'no, Lily isn't a lesbian', and 'yes, she is a good friend'. What might Jacek possibly have said?

She goes through the rigmarole of answering lame questions about her friends.

'Have you ever had a crush on Tonia Banda?' – "No, I'm straight," she says aloud.

'Would you trust Coral Hemming with your life?' – "Sure, why not?"

'Would you play naked Twister with Gregory McGoldrick?' – "No, he's my cousin…"

She finally has enough points to unlock some answers. The first two make her snort. The third dashes her hopes.

"He's lying," says Coral simply.

"He doesn't seem like a liar," sniffs Lily. "He was honest about the other two questions, even though they were sexual."

"Maybe Gabriela was right next to him when he got round to the last one?" suggests Coral, with unerring but unknown accuracy.

"I can't allow myself to hope that," says Lily softly. "It sucks so much! I always felt that there was undeniable chemistry between us… It seems that I was wrong. I thought that if he ever left Gabriela I'd have a chance, but not if he only sees me as a friend, or a sister. It makes me feel really flat."

"Aww," says Coral, opening her arms for a gratefully received hug.

Still, Lily thinks as she wanders to the bathroom for a soothing hot bath, at least Jacek thinks she's interesting. A skinny-dipping member of the Mile High Club! She giggles. Jacek knows by now that Lily is honest, but he probably won't believe her if she ever finds herself telling him that she's still a virgin…

Several weeks before, Lily's birthday flare-up was a resounding success. People tried to forget the dress code, but scarves proved necessary on that wet autumn evening; three people actually brought more interesting pyro than sparklers, and the display that Coral, a known pyrophobic, filmed from the bedroom window was a YouTube hit for weeks. The guests had spelled out "Arsenal" in fire and flames (and sparklers), some more reluctantly than others. Lily was particularly happy when she noticed that the famous video of Dinamo Zagreb fans spelling out 'Dinamo' in flares on a stand during a game was now a related link to her video.

Now, everyone is preparing for Christmas. Decorations are up in all the students' houses, although most of them won't get to look at them once term finishes on December the 9th. Lily plans to work for a week after term has finished and go home on the 16th.

Hope's Christmas party is on the last day of term. Sue Hill has booked a room at a local hotel, the Dolphin; tickets include

Christmas dinner, a disco, and karaoke. Lily loves to sing, and has known what she's going to sing for weeks. It is a love song. She's not sure whether it is a good thing or not that Jacek isn't going to be there.

The first full week of December comes around fast. Hilarity ensues at work as Arsenal qualify from their Champions League group, while Manchester United do not. Jacek can quickly silence Lily by referring to League position, but is visibly wound up about the exit, which gives Lily and the other ABUs – Anything But Uniteds – at work a bit of fun.

On the day of the party, Lily says goodbye to her friends; Heidi is going back to Leeds, Tonia to Portsmouth, Coral to London – she's a truer Arsenal fan than Lily, really. Lily plans to spend her time alone in the house wrapping presents, praying, watching TV, making mince pies and chocolate Christmas puddings for work and to take home. She is a little lonely, but content in the knowledge that work will fill much of her time, and in a few short days she will be home.

That Friday, after prayer and a serious baking session, she gets ready to go out. She has decided to wear a dress that she bought in 2010 for a Bullet For My Valentine gig. It is a multi-purpose dress, part goth, part glamour; a corset top, black, laced with white elastic, and a full skirt, black on top, red underneath, with an inch of solid red silky fabric showing proudly at the bottom. It falls just above knee length. Lily tones down the gothic element by pairing it with barely noticeable tights, patent red shoes with pointy toes and a small heel, and a feathery black cardigan, cropped to the waist. Lily is modest, and fully accepting of her average-attractive status, but even she cannot deny that tonight she looks fantastic.

In the Bogdanowski flat, things are not going smoothly. Gabriela and Jacek have had one of their periodic rows, this time about the cat. Jacek's cat predates Gabriela's arrival; he bought her for company when he first arrived in England. Her name is Malinka, meaning 'little raspberry'. No, she isn't pink, or even red. She's a dark tortoiseshell, orange at best. Jacek just liked the name.

"She sleeps on the bed," says Gabriela in Polish. "We agreed that she would not."

"Yes, but I can't watch her all the time," argues Jacek. "I work, and I shut the bedroom door when I go out. You must have forgotten to do the same."

"I forgot because I work two jobs and I'm bloody tired!"

"That was your choice. You can't blame me or the cat for the consequences."

"I didn't have a choice. You spend all our money!"

"Since when did we have a joint account? I spend all my money, and you spend all yours." It looks like a long evening ahead.

Lily arrives at the Dolphin Hotel to cheers and wolf-whistles from her impressed colleagues. Feeling confident she takes a twirl in front of them. She loves what her dress does for her.

"Wow, if I had your legs…" says Lynn admiringly.

"You do have my legs. You're an inch taller than me, and very skinny."

"Yeah, but I don't like my knees, or my veins."

"Tights are for veins, and I don't like my knees either. Trust me, Lynn, when you're actually too old to dress like this, you'll regret not doing it now!"

Jane Austen fan Janet is listening to the conversation, and is oddly reminded of Miss Elizabeth Bennett, for young Lily does indeed give her opinion very freely, considering her age. Unlike Lady Catherine de Burgh, Lynn and Janet are not offended, but impressed by Lily's maturity and positivity. This admiration often comes across as surprise, leaving Lily acutely aware of how different she is, which she doesn't always like very much.

Dinner is delicious – turkey for the majority, but Lily, though not a vegetarian, is not a fan of turkey, and opted for salmon with new potatoes and green beans when the menus were passed around at work. Janet, who is a vegetarian, gets a vegetable Wellington with a rich tomato sauce. Everyone but the hardened carnivores is slightly jealous.

"I'd have had that if it wasn't for my outfit," confesses Lily. "I thought pastry might make me look pregnant, and in any case, I want dessert!"

Lily's family has a tradition of keeping a Christmas pudding and having it after Easter dinner. Lily would eat it every day if she could.

Meanwhile, a few miles away…

"You bought a ticket to the work do, but you aren't going?"

"Yes. I don't feel like it," says Gabriela. She and Jacek managed to put feline difference behind them, and are now on the sofa in front of a classic Polish film whose title translates as "How I Started the Second World War".

Suddenly, Jacek is feeling torn. He wonders anew why he eschews socialising. In the beginning, living with Gabriela was exciting, and he wanted to stay in all the time and do coupley things – snuggle on the sofa, play board games or PlayStation, make love in every room. Since then, Gabriela has come to expect Jacek to be in every night. Gabriela cooks, ergo Jacek must clean, and she does not like dishes to be left until morning. A typical discussion about Jacek going out would go like this:

"I am thinking of going to the Polish club to watch Legia-Wisla tonight."

"But you can watch that here."

"Yes, but you don't like football, and it clashes with things you do like."

"What time is it at?"

"5pm. Finishing around 6.45."

"Oh…"

"What?"

"Nothing, it's just that I bought fresh stuff for dinner, and it'll go off if we don't have it today.

"We could have a late dinner."

"Will you want to do the dishes late?"

Jacek, like Lily, is honest and self-aware. "No, I don't suppose I will."

He likes to sit and digest his dinner, watch some TV, and then head for bed, preferably not alone. Chores do not belong to the late evening.

"Okay, I'll stay here. Do you mind me watching?"

"No, I'll tape Hollyoaks. Thanks for being so understanding, Jacek."

Jacek likes to please Gabriela, and does not like arguments; thus his days have become structured around her needs. Just recently, however, arguments have become part of the fabric of domestic life, and he has begun to realise – from colleagues' stories, from friends' Facebooks, from the amazing YouTube video of Lily's birthday that has had 14,000 hits – just how much he is missing out on.

"How would you feel if I went?"

"Fine. The dishes are done."

Dishes! thinks Jacek as he puts on more presentable clothes than his Iron Maiden T-shirt and jeans with a hole in the knee – a black shirt, black trousers, smart but understated black slip-on shoes. (He looks amazing in black.) But, seriously, *dishes!* Why is a nineteen-year-old woman so keen to chain him to the sink? Why is she so domesticated? At her age, he was out on the tiles most nights. He first met Gabriela in a bar; he assumed from her presence there that she must be fun loving, and indeed, for the first few months, they partied rather than dated. Since he asked her to move in, however… Actually, the signs were there before. He asked her to move in partly because he loved her, partly because the lease was up on her flat and her flatmate Madzia was going back to Poland, but mostly because she'd started to decline his offers of nights out. She made it clear that she loved him, but "wasn't really into all this hard partying"; he'd been spending an increasing amount of time on her sofa, and it made sense, once they'd been together a year and she had nowhere to live, to transfer the relationship to his own sofa. He was happy with this arrangement, or so he had always though, until the arguments had begun.

Even now, he puts most of the rows down to a natural evolution of domesticity – the easy part is over. It's the same for every relationship, he realises, and you can't chop and change every time someone doesn't appreciate your cat, or your smoking, or your underwear drying in the bathroom, or your inability to cook. Jacek is a peaceful and generous man; were he not, he would have asked Gabriela whose flat it was at least once by now.

Another explanation he has for the rows is the onset of winter. Before September, before the days had closed down and the nights spread out to fill the void, he had ignored or tolerated Gabriela's hen-pecking. He knows that he gets grumpy in winter; a resultant Goth phase in his mid-teens led to the revelation that he looks amazing in black. In spring, he will stop snapping back; until then, he will try. It will be his New Year's resolution, and he will start early. With this in mind, he goes to the living room to give Gabriela a big kiss and hug before heading out into the night. She's fallen asleep on the sofa, so instead, he kisses her forehead and pulls a rug over her. He hopes that she felt it, and that she knows he meant it.

6

The dancing is full steam ahead at the Dolphin Hotel. Lily is dancing with Jim, who has said "sorry" at least three times, and promised to buy her a new pair of shoes to replace the ones he has trampled to death. Janet and her husband are doing proper dancing, with steps and stuff, not just twirling randomly like everyone else. Sue and Derek Hill are moving exuberantly; their table contains two empty bottles of wine and Sally, who has had half a glass of white, and is now doing her party trick of sitting and looking disapproving.

"Why has she come?" whispers Lynn mischievously to her dance partner, Frank from security, who has wrested himself from the clutches of Veronica Trollope. Lily's decision to dance with Jim was made partly so that Veronica would know jealousy as well as her husband.

"Right," comes a booming voice over the speakers, which belongs to David Hope. "I hope everyone's having a good time" – drunken cheers, a "Hmph" from Sally Hill – "and is ready for the karaoke competition!"

"They never told us it was a competition," dithers Lynn, chewing on her lip. "I might not sing now."

"Don't be ridiculous," grins Frank. "I bet you have a lovely voice." He doesn't need to say it, though. Lynn is already thinking of Lily's words about regret. Tonight might be the only opportunity she gets to do something so juvenile and fun; it's not something her social circle of middle-aged mums would contemplate.

David continues, "Competitors should form a line by the DJ booth. No need for slips – he knows his catalogue like the back of his hand. He'll just take your name, and two choices of songs. First come, first served if any of you want to sing the same song. Off you go!"

"Excuse me, Jim," says Lily, but in the end he follows her to the karaoke booth – his party-piece is singing 'Blueberry Hill'.

Everyone knows that the competition is pointless because the winner will be Hazel from Home Shopping. Lily likes Hazel. She is thirty four years old, has two degrees, a TEFL certificate and a passport full of exotic stamps. Having been made redundant during the recession, she took the first job she could find to continue saving money for her final fling, a wine-tasting tour of the world. If Lily is Elizabeth Bennett, then Hazel is an older Georgiana Darcy, full of impressive accomplishments. She plays guitar in a Nightwish-style metal band, but can sing any kind of music. Tonight, she has gone for 'Come In Out of the Rain'. It will be note-perfect.

As singers come and go – some good, some awful – Lily becomes nervous. Frank gets a big cheer for 'You Sexy Thing' – he looks exactly like Errol Brown, so it's more Stars In Their Eyes than X Factor. Lynn nervously but tunefully sings 'La Isla Bonita'. Neil and Pat from Human Resources murder 'Don't Stop Me Now', their girlfriends killing themselves laughing. Lydia sings half of 'Lola's Theme' before realising she doesn't know the words, and walking off giggling to finish her glass of rosé.

After Jim's excellent rendition of Blueberry Hill, his 1950s crooning filling the room and making everybody look up in surprise, comes Hazel. Those who have heard her sing before know what to expect. Her voice is astonishingly high, yet she manages to get enough projection on the lower notes for them to be not only audible, but also spine-tinglingly sultry. The last chorus is in a ridiculously high key, but she doesn't falter. Lily's one criticism is that Hazel's voice is maybe slightly churchy in a white way, and doesn't have the right timbre for the song. This is extreme nitpicking, though, and nobody really wants to nitpick. Hazel gets a standing ovation.

"Well, I think a star is born there!" booms the DJ into his microphone. "Next up is Lily McGoldrick from Grocery, singing 'Save The Best For Last' by Vanessa Williams. Give her a big hand, ladies and gentlemen… Oh, I say, I do like your dress. Does it come in a size 22?" asks the DJ, who is rather large and very camp.

Lily stumbles to the front of the stage, accepts a microphone, takes a deep breath, and begins. Her voice is a tone or two lower than Hazel's, and wobbles a little over the first few notes, but soon finds the clarity needed for a slow song without much variation in pitch:

'Sometimes the snow comes down in June
Sometimes the sun goes round the moon
I see the passion in your eyes
Sometimes it's all a big surprise…'

The staff of Hope Stores appreciate the fact that they have seen three good singers in a row. People have started to dance to the sound of their colleagues' efforts: Sue with her head on Derek's shoulder, Neil and Pat holding pretend microphones and indulging in overacting, and Jim with Veronica, who may just have learned her lesson.

Jacek enters the hotel, puts his coat in the cloakroom, and enters the hall just as Lily is entering her favourite part of the song:

''Cos how could you give your love to someone else
And share your dreams with me?
Sometimes the very thing you're looking for
Is the one thing you can't see…'

She sees Jacek at this point and, impressively, manages to give him a shy wave and carry on singing, rather than dropping the microphone and giggling. Jacek waves back. He has heard every word, although the song is only familiar to him via Wave 105 at work, and suddenly, a kind of dreadful clarity dawns upon him.

It is not winter that has made him start arguing with Gabriela, nor the decline of their once fun relationship into humdrum domesticity. There is only one reason he even noticed the boring nature of his life, and she arrived just as the days closed down and the nights spread out to fill the void. She woke him up to the inadequacy of his home life by being young and lively and sparky and trying to include him in her social circle – not to mention by being beautiful. Granted, Lily is not as likely as Gabriela to be snapped up by a modelling agency, but she does have perfect skin and hair, a cute gap-toothed smile, a superb size 10 figure, good legs *and* a half-decent chest – how often did you see that combination? Put simply, Lily gets, at worst, a B+ for looks and an A+ for personality, versus Gabriela's A+ for looks and, at best, B minus for the other… Well, there is no doubt as to who is maintaining a higher GPA.

Jacek is torn down the middle. He has never felt like this before; he has always known exactly what he wants in life and love. *You can't just pack Gabriela in,* says a voice in the back of his head. *Love isn't as rational as you're trying to be in your assessment and, for whatever reason, you love her.*

But did lovers compromise as much as he had to fit into Gabriela's idea of how to do life?

He needs to get out of there. He inwardly curses Lily for providing such a dark temptation. She is his friend, and he ought to be able to go over there and give her a hug and congratulate her on her performance, but he can't. To work out what he really feels, he has to be far away from her. He turns tail and leaves, forgetting his coat entirely.

Lily is trembling with exhilaration. The song is over, she sang it really well and, to put the icing on the cake, Jacek heard her! Does he realise she listens to that song whenever her feelings for him are particularly intense, whenever sleep flies away because the pleasure in her chest gets too strong? He has shared his dreams with her, although Lily is the more open of the two, and he surely must know that Lily fits him much better than Gabriela. But then Lily remembers that he doesn't think she's hot. How important that is, she thinks sadly. She has had situations in her life in which a perfectly nice, intelligent, right-on guy has become besotted with her – and there's just nothing there one her side. How cruel Cupid often is, to strike a person with longing, but ignore the object of the longing!

Jacek, halfway home, is really messed up now. He thought, naively perhaps, that getting out of the intense atmosphere of the party, away from the siren who seemed to be serenading him, would solve everything. He is seized by an unfamiliar fear; What if he is so desperate to know his feelings for each woman that he psychologically self-destructs and feels nothing for either of them anymore? His melancholy brother used to complain of such afflictions… No, I am not like Arkadiusz, he tells himself firmly. If any such thing happened, it would be temporary. I am in control of my feelings, in a good way.
Am I? *Well, no, but that kind of self-destruction doesn't seem like me. Feeling nothing – no, Feeling a contradictory splurge of too much – yes.*

Back at the party, Lily wonders where Jacek has gone.

"I saw him go out, but he left his cloak in the cloakroom," says Janet.

"Gone for a fag, probably," says Lynn. "Think I'll join him."

"No – wait for the results!" implores Lily as David Hope takes centre stage once again.

"Well, I know I'm having a good time tonight. How about everybody else?"

More drunken cheering.

"I have the results of the karaoke competition," announces David. "In last place, winning one of Hope Stores' *most* durable wooden spoons – Neil Casey and Pat Myers for their highly entertaining, if sadly lacking, rendition of 'Don't Stop Me Now'."

Neil and Pat lurch to the front and insinuate sexual acts with the wooden spoon.

"In third place, for his resonant version of 'Blueberry Hill' – Jim Trollope!"

Everyone gets to their feet; Jim is shocked. He has no idea his voice is even half-decent, although it gets enough appreciation on New Year's Eve and down the Labour Club on Fridays.

Second place is always the most exciting award, thanks to Hazel's monopolisation of first, and this year, there is more competition for it than usual.

"In second place, plus winning the award for Best Newcomer, which I just made up on the spot, is Lily McGoldrick for her angelic performance of 'Save the Best for Last'!"

Lily is genuinely surprised – unlike everyone else in the room – and thrilled. She strides up to the stage, grinning from ear to ear, to accept her prize of a hand-held blender. Good job she cooks. *What if Jacek had won it?,* she thinks. *Where is he, anyway?*

"Don't pine too much, honey," grins Sue, reading Lily's thoughts as usual. "I'm sure he'll be done with the cancer sticks soon enough, and come and congratulate you."

As Hazel is crowned the winner – Lily cheers extra hard, aware that people don't always appreciate Hazel because she's the Manchester United of the karaoke world, which doesn't seem as fair as hating Manchester United – Jacek is pushing the key into his front door. There is still too much Lily in his system for his liking.

Gabriela is no longer on the sofa. Jacek goes up to look at her in bed. The bedroom is spotless. All the furnishings and decorations, except his one Dragonforce poster, were brought by Gabriela from her previous flat. Jacek recognises a feeling he has had for a long time, but has been unable to name; alienation. In the past, when going through a rough period, Jacek sometimes hated coming home after a night at a friend's house; the stress and anxiety he had been feeling seemed to lie in wait for him among his possessions. Being at home was no longer a homely feeling. He feels something similar now. His life and Gabriela's have become one, but he is not comfortable with this. They are not married, after all. Perhaps his mother is right and you shouldn't live with a girlfriend before marriage. It seems to work for almost everyone he knows, though.

Anyway, he doesn't feel bad, just uncomfortable. What is the difference between how he felt bad about his bedroom in the past, and how he feels funny about it now?

In a flash, he knows the answer. In a word – sex. He has sex in there, with Gabriela, which hides a multitude of sins. Is that all love is, then – sex? Reconciling one's differences in the bedroom? Isn't that a bit mad? But then the feeling rather than the state, that he knows as love, separate from sex – the difference between loving and being in love, although Jacek isn't sure which one is which – is anything but rational.

Does he have it for Gabriela? Not in its former glory. Does he have it for Lily?

"I need a beer," he evades aloud, in Polish. He goes to the fridge, where a blue Post-It note that wasn't there before catches his attention.

'Jacek, you forgot to wash the slow-cooker.'

"I DON'T CARE!" he suddenly roars, and equally suddenly, everything seems clear. He goes outside. It is December. It is the coldest night of the year so far. He doesn't really notice.

7

Lily has given up on finding Jacek, which means her sleep is likely to be disturbed by unresolved anticipation. Did she manage to move him at all?

"You're thinking like it was something you set out to do," she scolds herself on the way home. "You didn't even know he was going to be there."

To be honest, him turning up like that was literally a fantasy come true. She'd imagined him walking through the door, hearing the words that were always intended for him, and realising in his heart that there were never two people so clearly made for each other as Lily and Jacek. She will have to wait until Monday to find out if is has worked at all. She gets ready for bed quickly and decides to read until her eyes are heavy.

Ding-dong.

What?, thinks Lily, half-awake with a book in her hand and her reading light on. The doorbell? Has she dreamed it? Probably. But, just in case…

Ding-dong. It rings again as she's halfway to the window to see if there's anyone out there. Who on earth could it be?, she wonders. Was Heidi's coach cancelled and she's come back from London? Wouldn't she go to her own flat? But maybe she left her own keys with Tonia, or the landlady…

When Lily opens the door on the chain, she's not far off the correct height to look at: Heidi is five feet nine inches tall, and from there to six feet isn't far.

"Jacek! What are you doing here? You must be freezing!"

Her heart rate immediately accelerates, and a wall of heat washes over her like a tidal wave. This happens every single day at work. How can a bodily response be so enduring?

Jacek's answer is silent. He walks into the hall, closes the door behind him, turns towards Lily, and kisses her. Soft on the lips, three times; no tongues, but definitely not friendly kisses.

"Jacek!" says Lily breathlessly, falling back against the wall. "What about Gabri…"

"I've left her. Come here. You're so fucking beautiful. Why didn't I see it before?" He kisses her again, in the same way.

Something explodes from that beautiful part of Lily's chest that she's got to know so well. Empowered, in love and blissfully happy, she finally kisses him back. It is, and feels, emphatic and fantastic. No more repression, no holding back. She has Jacek Bogdanowski in her arms. What is she going to do about it?

* * *

"Lily, do you have a condom?"

"No. No, I don't. I'm a virgin."

Jacek knows by now that Lily doesn't lie. He sits up and looks deep into her eyes, blue into green.

"Do you want me to take your virginity?"

Please, God, Lily silently prays. *I can't answer no to this question. Maybe I shouldn't have made myself vulnerable like this, but... Well, you know how I feel about him. If this isn't right, please stop us. In Jesus' name, Amen.*

She nods at Jacek, who nods back and pushes her onto the bed…

He intends to withdraw, given their lack of protection. However, for a man who has sex a lot, he seems to have forgotten what sex feels like. First sex, of course – whether first ever, or first time with someone new – is a different kettle of fish from couple-sex, however loving. He is on fire. He knows he must be gentle with Lily, but franticness threatens to take hold. He knows his ability to be sensible may have been compromised, but not until Lily starts to come does he realise how incapable of sense he is, and joins her.

"Oh God, Jacek, I love you," she cries as he collapses on top of her. "Sorry if that's too much."

She is in tears. Jacek is astounded. While he is unselfish in bed, he has never considered himself a man whose lovemaking prowess can shatter a woman to such an extent.

"Never too much, Lily," he says in his usual Slavonic growl, kissing her. "Never are you too much. Don't worry…"

He falls asleep inside her, soothed and satisfied beyond both expectation and explanation.

8

Lily wakes up. Oh, but it was not a dream! Oh, but Jacek Bogdanowski is lying on top of her! What a beautiful day, feeling and sight! She kisses his shoulder and neck. She will not wake him by force, but will leave it to his nervous system by providing just a little stimulation, just a tease.

He is coming to. She smoothes down his back muscles, easing his transition into the real world. "Good morning, Jacek."

"Mmm, Lily," he murmurs. He is still inside her. "Do I have to leave? It's so comfortable here."

They both giggle at his double-entendre. "No. You can stay for as long as you like, Jacek. Make yourself at home."

He does. It is the best morning ever.

It is the best afternoon ever. They huddle in bed and watch TV, kissing each other whenever things are to quiet, or the BBC's Saturday sports coverage is of something daft, like curling. They play-fight in bed when one of their teams scores, or doesn't score, but both Arsenal and Manchester United win, which feels to both Jacek and Lily like an affirmation of their fledgling relationship. Jacek pulls out his phone to order pizza.

"But it's the end of term. I can't aff…" pleads Lily.

He silences her with a kiss and orders, "Menu." This means she has to get up, which she doesn't like, but she does like Jacek's clear appreciation of her naked walk to the bedroom door.

"Ass of an angel," he purrs. When she returns, he massages her bottom and kisses it all over…

Later, Jacek pretends he has heard a scooter draw up when he hasn't yet. He has to do what he has told Lily he has already done.

"You can't just stay out all night," snaps Gabriela in lieu of "Hi, Jacek".

"Yes, I can," says Jacek brusquely. "It's over."

"I beg your pardon?"

"Gabriela," he sighs, more kindly, "we have not been getting on for a while. Do you agree?"

"No! What is this?"

Something I didn't expect, thinks Jacek grimly.

"Gabi, listen. We argue all the time. You don't let me go out. You run my flat. That would have been my first night out alone in nine months, but when I started to think bad things about you, I came home to try to make myself realise that it's you I love." His voice hardens a little, as does his heart. "And then I found your note on the fridge."

"You dumped me because you don't like cleaning the slow cooker?"

He can hear the catch in her voice. *She's a child,* he realises, *an immature baby.*

"No, Gabriela. I dumped you because you are always telling me how to live in my own flat. Now, I think maybe you can stay there. It's more yours than mine. However, I would like you to stay with a friend on Sunday. I will come at 8pm to move out my things, and stay there for the night."

Jacek plans to take up a long-standing offer to live with his friend Marko, a Croatian musician who Jacek used to play drums for every once in a while, and who is looking for help with the rent. The doorbell rings.

"Sorry, Gabriela, I need to go. We can talk more some other time. Good luck, and I'm sorry. Really, I am."

Jacek feels a pang in his chest as he ends the call. *Still, could have been a worse boyfriend,* he thinks. Could have ended the phone call with, "Pizza's here, sorry, bye." Could have sent her a text or email. Could have moved his stuff out last night, and never left her verbally at all.

Lily's bedroom is like a magical cove. As soon as he's there, with two steaming boxes of stuffed crust, the pang fades to a wheedle. He is pretty sure Lily can fix wheedles.

"I feel a little bad for Gabriela," he admits.

Lily takes his hand. "Did you try to make it work?"

The list of his compromises, and the times he backed down, won't fit on a single page of his brain.

"Yes."

"Well, then," says Lily. "Leaving someone always feels bad, and I always cry… Well, I did the one time he didn't leave me."

"Why would anybody leave you?" Jacek asks in astonishment, looking mostly at Lily's bare chest.

"Gabriela's better looking than me, but you're here with me," points out Lily. "It's all about personality and chemistry. What clicks? I'd say you and I click pretty well. But, if you still feel bad about it…" Lily places her hands on Jacek's chest, and a firm kiss upon his lips. "Pizza's better cold, anyway," she giggles, as Jacek finds his way to the place where he feels unsettled, wonderful and safe.

It is the best evening ever. Lily insists on going to the pub.

"I'd forgotten what they look like," admits Jacek.

For fear of meeting Gabriela, they eschew Lily's beloved local, the Mitre, and walk the short distance to the Rockstone, holding hands. Having sat in blissful silence for most of the day, they fall over themselves to talk. There were never any awkward moments between Lily and Jacek. She meets some uni friends, and introduces them to her "new boyfriend". The day couldn't have gone any better if Lily had scripted it herself. When they return to Lily's, they fall into bed and make love as if their lives depend on it.

On Sunday morning, Lily kisses Jacek's forehead to wake him. "I'm going to church," she whispers. "Coming?"

"Nn-nn," Jacek mutters. "Have fun."

"I'll be back with breakfast," Lily promises.

No day has ever been as bright as this Sunday morning. The British public tend to greet each other on Sunday mornings as they do not at other times, and Lily does so exuberantly.

She doesn't quite know how to feel in church, so she says, *God, I'm sorry if I've sinned against you with Jacek. If you want me to stop doing it, you'll have to intervene. A lot. But thank you so, so much for bringing us together. I'm going to praise you for that now. In Jesus' name I pray, Amen.*

She worships with all her heart during the service. She feels inclined to promise not to have sex with Jacek for the rest of the day, but can't bring herself to do so. She therefore leaves it in God's hands, and goes to the Co-op for goodies.

As it turns out, God is listening. Jacek seems to know, instinctively, that Lily will feel bad if she misbehaves directly after church on a Sunday. They eat breakfast in bed, then give each other long, sensual back massages, the pleasure in Lily's chest unabating as she relaxes Jacek's body with her hands, just as she once imagined. Totally at peace, they can barely stand to drag themselves to Varsity 2 for a late Sunday lunch and back-to-back football matches, but they somehow manage.

Afterwards, Jacek is loath to leave Lily, but he collects his bag from her flat and heads to that which was once his for the last time. They share a long, precious kiss at her door, which gets Lily ridiculously hot and bothered, given how many times she released such feelings on Saturday, and agree to see each other at work the next day as part of a giggly, covert couple.

But you have noticed the thickness of the book in your hand, right?

9

Jacek pushes open his front door and gasps in astonishment. His flat has been Jaceked. His favourite posters are back on the wall – Halle Berry, a series of funny road signs edited to be about drunkenness, Manchester United (of course). His drum kit is reassembled – badly – in the place where Gabriela's pink inflatable chair once sat. His favourite jumper is on the back of the sofa, where he used to leave it for easy reach, before a tidy person moved in. He has not quite computed how this must have happened by the time Gabriela walks into the room.

"Please don't be angry with me," she begs. "You were right. I took advantage of your good nature, and it was me deciding everything. If you really don't love me, I will leave now, and you can move out – or I will. I don't mind. But if there is even a chance that we can still be together, please stay, Jacek. I love you."

The pain in Jacek's chest, so anaesthetised by Lily and her charms, becomes so sharp that it cannot be ignored, and something inside him stirs as he looks at Gabriela. He feels as if he is on the horns of a dilemma, whilst, deep down, he knows what he must do, and hates himself for having made such a big mess.

Does he love Gabriela? Maybe.

Does he love Lily? Maybe.

Does he like Lily, and dislike Gabriela, enough to tell the latter that in spite of her obvious repentance and willingness to work on the relationship, there is definitely no hope for the couple, and they should cut their losses now and move on?

If he says yes, and it doesn't work out with Lily, he will always wonder. How can the same world, the same lives, seem so different here from just down the road?

"Okay, Gabriela, listen to me," he sighs. "I love you. I do not know if I am in love with you. Or maybe the other way round. I know this must hurt you a lot. I feel confused and broken, but I am willing to give us another chance, and I am touched by how much you want me to stay. Is that enough for you?"

Gabriela sniffs and nods. "Yes. I promise I will do all I can to make you feel better. If you decide, any time, that you do not love me, I will let you go."

"I suppose," says Jacek thoughtfully, "that if I did not love you at all, I would be unable to fight the uncontrollable urge to do this."

He takes Gabi in his arms and kisses her, then holds her close as she bursts into tears.

"Oh, Gabriela, forgive me," he whispers, his own eyes beginning to blink and blur.

Oh, Lily, forgive me, he mentally begs. Extricating himself from Gabriela, he says, "One moment, please. I have a very important phone call to make. Then I'm all yours."

Lily sighs, a deep, mournful breath. "I think you're right. She does deserve a chance. I think you're noble and honourable and honest and doing the right thing. I suppose if you weren't so perfect, I wouldn't be sad right now."

"I am not perfect," growls Jacek, who has never felt less perfect.

"You're as close as makes no difference. Listen, Jacek, I'm your friend, and I'm not your only friend. If you ever feel like you did on Friday again, please go and talk to someone neutral about how you feel. This isn't a telling off, and I know how hard you men find it to confide in each other, but… please try."

After agreeing that she and Jacek will remain firm friends and will never talk about what happened again, Lily hangs up, and promptly bursts into tears. However, they are just hot tears of shock, and are soon gone. She realises that it is definitely better to have loved and lost than never to have loved at all. Yes, she'll feel bad for a week or so, but then it will all just be fantastic memories. One thing's for sure – she and Jacek will never lose touch. You can't share that much love, and part that amicably, without becoming BFFs – best friends forever.

The next day, Lily wakes up feeling a dull ache in the stomach, close to the place that feels pleasure when she thinks about love. She wishes she didn't have to go to work, but she does, and it isn't too bad. She and Jacek share a quick friendly hug in the empty canteen, and he looks into her green eyes and apologises once more.
"Are you all right?" he asks, sincerely.
She nods, gives his waist a final squeeze, and goes down to work.

Lily hasn't quite survived the weekend's emotional rollercoaster unscathed, and feels more vulnerable than usual; the bad moods of harassed Christmas customers don't help at all. On Wednesday, a foul-mouthed older gentleman who can't find the right sized pot of pickled onions accosts Lily.

"You young people are nothing but lazy fuckers! You're not lifting a finger to help me!" She has single-handedly carried two huge trays of jars out of the storeroom, for him to choose an appropriate size. "And don't look at me like that, you little slag." She is not looking at him at all. "I'd like to speak to your manager, please."

She hands the irritant over to Raj, Sally's line manager, runs away, and bursts into tears. She had begun to feel a gnawing sense of guilt about surrendering her virginity. Guilt is not a welcome addition to her latent pain. She goes to ride it out in the canteen, but is diverted en route by Sue.

"Oh, sweetheart, what's wrong?"

"Stupid customer. Sorry. I wasn't in a good mood anyway."

Sue shepherds Lily into an empty training room. "Something happened, didn't it? Between you and *him*?"

"How do you know these things?" gulps Lily. "You mustn't say anything to anyone!"

"Wouldn't dream of it, dear. He's gone back to Gabi, though, hasn't he?" She tuts. "Bad move, if you ask me. You're ten times the woman she is."

"Thanks, but it's because he's so nice that he's given her a chance. He couldn't have lived with his conscience if he hadn't. There's more to him than meets the eye."

Sue's own eyes have gone a little dreamy and glazed. "All that and beautiful too? No wonder you don't feel so good. Would you like to take the rest of the week off?"

Lily shakes her head. "Thanks, but I'd rather not sit around and mope. Jacek and I are cool with each other. It's just the abuse I was getting off this customer."

Lily and Sue return to the fray. On the way, they have the pleasure of seeing the offended customer being physically removed from the store by Frank and Jim. He's hurling racial abuse at Frank and Raj, and being told thoroughly off by old ladies on all sides as a result. One of them takes a swing at him with her handbag. Lily would loved to have had a video camera… Would she get away with conspiring with the security lads to put the CCTV footage on YouTube?, she wonders, feeling a heck of a lot better all of a sudden.

10

Christmas doesn't make Lily forget Jacek completely, but she has a good time nonetheless. Family, friends and lots and lots of food are powerful distractions, and if 'Lonely This Christmas' ever comes on the radio, she just turns it off. Anyway, she's not lonely; she just hasn't got a boyfriend, which is no different from seventeen of the twenty one previous Christmases she has known. That doesn't stop her from standing by her bedroom window on a beautiful Christmas Eve and whispering, "Merry Christmas, darling, wherever you are," before blowing a kiss in the direction of Southampton Water. Come to think of it, he might actually be in Poland, rendering the action pointless, but it's the thought that counts. Soppy things and Christmas go hand in hand, though, provided they aren't allowed to take over.

She returns to Southampton in early January. Amazingly, she arrives seconds after Coral, or so she thinks. Coral is on the doorstep, but has actually been there for fifteen minutes, trying to extract her key, which has broken off and stuck in the door.

"Yours won't go in if I can't get mine out," says Coral desperately. "I phoned the landlord, but he can't get here until 8pm." It is 5.30. "Shall we go for a pint?"

"Sure, why not?... Oh, wait, no, we've got loads of money!" Their student loan cheques came a week beforehand. "How about a curry?"

Curry seems like a wonderful idea until the next morning, when Lily and Coral both throw up.

"Chicken!" groans Coral. "I keep saying I'll never order chicken when I'm out again. This is the third time I've had food poisoning."

"I had lamb," Lily points out. "It must be poor food hygiene in general. When you're a literary historian, and I'm something wonderful" – Lily has lots of ideas for her future, but has no clue which one is The One – "we'll eat at expensive places, and hopefully they'll be cleaner."

Lily was meant to be going to work, but the rules say you have to wait twenty four hours after having vomited before coming into work. She goes to work on Tuesday, but is throwing up in the toilets within an hour. The week continues with a similar pattern – or lack of one. Just as she thinks the food poisoning is gone, it strikes again, and Lily manages a grand total of four hours' work.

"Well, you've never taken a day's holiday," says Sue. "I'll put every day that you have to go home down as holiday, then you'll be paid." Hope's only offers sick pay to those on long-term sick leave, and even then, it is a tiny proportion of what people would get if they were well enough to work.

"I think you should stop trying to go to work and relax," advises Coral on Thursday. "Our reading lists for next week are here – you could crack on. At least you wouldn't be walking around."

She is at the computer, checking her university email. She will probably never do so again – twice a year, at the beginning of the semester, is the norm, and Lily and all her friends are due to graduate in May.

Coral's advice is good. Lily has done all the reading for the first two weeks of term by Saturday, and has stopped throwing up. On Saturday afternoon, Coral runs up to use the loo before the girls go to the pub, and comes down looking like she has seen a ghost.

"Lils?"

"Coz?"

"I noticed something in the bathroom…"

"A big spider? Ugh, I don't like catching them either – I wonder if Heidi…"

"No, Lily," says Coral. She is trembling. "I've lived with you for two years, and I could be wrong here, but I've never gone away for the holidays and come back to find the same unopened packet of your STs on the laundry bin."

"Wow, that's… observant," says Lily, knowing she would never notice such a thing, and implying that therefore, Coral is sad.

"What I'm *trying* to say is that it's a bit funny that you were sick for a week after Sunday, and I was sick once, if we both caught the same poor hygiene bug."

Of course, the first thing Lily did after Jacek left her duplex apartment on that fateful Sunday was phone Coral; and she phoned Coral again, an hour later, when he *left her* left her. Coral knows everything, and has a point; Lily didn't come on when she was home for Christmas. She didn't even notice; she doesn't keep track.

"Right," says Lily slowly. "Well, I'm irregular, and I have missed odd ones, but I do think this is too many coincidences for me not to do a test. Best skip the pub and go to Boots."

"I'll come with you," says Coral immediately.

*   *   *

Lily stands and looks at herself in the mirror, takes a deep breath, and practices her speech again.

"Mum, Dad, I have always told you the truth. Every time you asked me if I'm a virgin, and I said yes, it was true. However, last term, someone swept me off my feet, and I had sex, and now I'm pregnant."

Indeed, she is. With a lot of memory jogging from Coral, she has remembered that she was last 'on' on the 29th of November.

"You wouldn't go swimming with Tonia, remember? She said why don't you use tampons, and you said they were uncomfortable, and she said you need to practice, and you said, 'What, right now?', and she took the hint and went with Heidi instead."

The NHS website says that her baby is due on or near the 6th of September 2012. At least she will have graduated – if the pregnancy is uncomplicated enough for her to study.

"Good job I've already researched for my dissertation," Lily mutters, before offering up a desperate prayer and pulling out her phone. The first call will be the hardest.

"Jacek, I'm pregnant."

His world spins around. "You're sure?"

"Yes. I'm over two weeks late and the test is positive. I'm so sorry. I should have insisted that we stop."

She doesn't quite mean it. On the whole, she'd rather take the past as it is, and be pregnant, than never have known Jacek in the way she did, but that's easy for her to say. She's single.

"Then I will need to tell Gabriela about us…"

You wonderful man, Lily thinks. *No are-you-going-to-get-rid-of-it, no secrets and lies. If only you could be my husband, as well as my child's father!* For the first time since December, she wants Jacek back with the strongest passion she has ever known.

"I'm sorry, Jacek."

"No, we were both responsible, and I am worse. You were single."

"So were you."

"You know what I mean." She does, although she doesn't *want* this to be any harder for Jacek than it is for her.

Jacek rings off, and goes to face Gabriela immediately. Her expression changes to one of concern as soon as she sees his face. He looks deep into her eyes, and takes a shuddering breath.

"My darling, when I left you, I slept with somebody else, and she is pregnant."

Gabriela gasps, and sinks into the sofa. "In twenty four hours, you slept with someone else?"

"Yes. I know I am a terrible man. You are free to leave me."

"I don't want to leave you! Go away! I need to think."

Jacek goes to the corner shop for cigarettes. When he returns, he finds Gabriela still on the sofa, pale and resolute.

"It's okay. You left me. You were free. I am surprised, but I asked for you back, and now I will deal with the consequences. Is she anyone I know?"

Jacek is glad she asked, and wishes he had told her straightaway. He should have collected his thoughts before going to talk to Gabriela.

"I should have said in the first place," admits Jacek. "I genuinely didn't think to. It is Lily."

Gabriela turns even paler. "Lily? You like her?"

"I thought I did… I mean – I do, as a person, but I thought I loved her. I ran from you to her. It was the worst thing I have ever done, and now I must be reminded of it for the rest of my life." He picks up his coat. "Do not hate Lily. She didn't pursue me. The fault is all mine. Now I must go and see her. It's only fair." He looks at the time. "I will be back in two hours. She lives above that big church, near Varsity. If I'm not back, come looking."

The only way he can think of to win back Gabriela's trust is to allow her to stalk him, if necessary.

Lily, meanwhile, is on the phone to her parents, saying exactly the words she has prepared.

"Thank you for telling me. I love you," says her mother. "Who is the father?"

Lily explains about Jacek. "I really thought he was the one, Mum," she says sadly. "I know I should at least have made him go out and buy a condom, but I was so caught up in the moment…"

"There but for the grace of God go I," says Lily's mum, who has always been honest about the risks she took as a young woman. "When am I going to become a grandmother?"

Jacek arrives at Lily's ten minutes later with a large bunch of pink and orange flowers. She puts them on the table; he hugs her tightly. There is no need to speak.

"I'm due next September," says Lily over cups of coffee. "Hopefully, I'll finish uni. I'm going to work really hard, try and get a First, and go straight into a PhD. When she's – I mean he or she – is old enough to go to nursery, I'll become a university lecturer."

"Is that what you want?" asks Jacek tenderly, unable to stop himself touching her hand.

"It was one of my options – not my first choice, but better than if I hadn't been to uni," says Lily firmly. "If I miss the grades, I'll do a PGCE and become a regular old teacher. Either way, I'll get the school holidays off."

They talk details for a while. Lily is going to keep her news quiet at work until she is the magical twelve weeks gone. Sue Hill will need to know for legal reasons, and so that Lily can be placed on light duties. Both Lily and Jacek will start savings accounts immediately.

"The worst thing is that my parents live in such an awkward place," laments Lily. "I'll phone the council on Monday and go on the council house waiting list for Southampton. I'll tell them I need to live here to give you adequate access to your child. I still might have to live on the Island for a couple of years, though."

"We'll find a way," says Jacek, simply and gravely, then it is time for him to leave.

Coral watches from the top of the stairs, then runs down and hugs Lily as she bursts into tears.

"I see what you mean," murmurs Coral into Lily's neck. "He is to *die* for."

"I'm a fucking idiot," grumbles Lily. "Let's go round to Heidi and Tonia's."

Both of Lily's other friends are immediately supportive.

"You're so lucky to have such a lovely mum," sighs Heidi. "Mine would kick me out."

"Mine would get me expelled from the church," says Tonia.

"Mine would go, 'Yay, a grandchild! Can you have it now? I can't wait!" says Coral, and everybody bursts into giggles, Lily loudest of all.

"So, Coral, is he all that?" asks Tonia when she hears that Jacek has been round to the house. Coral feigns fainting.

"I can see why our Lily was smitten," she admits.

"If he asked you to marry him, what would you say?" Heidi asks Lily.

"I would ask if he's absolutely sure he doesn't want to be with Gabriela," replies Lily decisively, and slightly wistfully.

"If he's sure, and I'm sure he's sure, I would scream, punch the air, and book the church. He's still perfect for me."

11

Lily has accepted her fate most graciously, but her body and mind have had a few too many shocks recently for all to be well. The first sign that something is amiss is excessive tiredness.

"Lily, you said you'd get up early to study today," whispers Coral. It is 11am on Thursday. Lily has changed her working hours due to the new university timetable, and has class at 1pm.

"I tried, but my limbs are just so heavy! I've never felt like this before. I thought you were supposed to get tired at two weeks pregnant, not four!"

"I don't know if it's that precise," muses Coral. "Here." She hands Lily a pile of books and a pad of paper from the desk opposite the bed. "Study in bed."

Unfortunately, Lily's concentration has been addled, too. "Come on, damn you, you need a First," she tells herself crossly. It doesn't help.

It also doesn't help that being pregnant means that the world is not Lily's oyster anymore, and that her paths are limited. She had no idea how much this would affect her psychologically. She can't go travelling at the end of the university year like she wanted to. In fact, she won't be able to until she's at least thirty-nine; probably in her forties. She won't be young and fit; she won't have a beach body. She won't have one this time next year, come to that. She might never find another man – didn't they tend to flee from single mums? She misses being Jacek's girlfriend with a passion that increases daily, and throughout it all, vicious internal voices are chanting, *'Shouldn't have done it. All your fault.'*

But she can't bring herself to own that she shouldn't have done something which, at the time, made her feel like the queen of the world. She also feels bad because she doesn't feel good about being pregnant; will she be able to love the baby at all? She does not want an abortion, but is she selfish not to consider adoption? But no; the baby is hers, and Jacek's, and she wants it…

The next Tuesday, Lily goes to work and lasts an hour. Mercifully, Gabriela and Jacek have a day off together. Lily woke up that morning and burst into tears. She fought them over breakfast, fought them walking down Portswood Road, and now, she fights them on the shop floor. At last, she can't even work. Everything she picks up feels like it weighs a ton, and she also has an uncomfortable sense of having to do the job perfectly, or something terrible will happen. She seeks out Sue.

"Can I go home, please? I just can't stop crying."

"Of course," says Sue immediately. "Do you want to talk?"

Lily shakes her head. "I'll go home and talk to my flatmate. I don't want to mess up your day."

As Lily leaves Sue's office, she notices that Sally is watching her curiously.

Coral is in bed when Lily gets home, and immediately shuffles over to make room for her.

"Okay, honey, what's wrong?"

Lily tells Coral everything she's been feeling as well as she can, which she doesn't feel is very well.

"Sweetheart, your hormones are all over the place, you've been rejected by someone you truly love, and your life has changed overnight. Of course you don't feel so good. I think you're doing very well. Why don't you try to go back to sleep?"

Sleep is mercifully swift to arrive, but come evening, Lily still has no energy, and is panicking. "I don't think I'll manage work tomorrow, or to do anything for uni," she babbles to an anxious Coral, who is sat on the edge of the bed she surrendered to Lily. "How am I supposed to support this kid if I can't finish my degree, or keep my job?"

"Calling in sick tomorrow won't kill you, and you don't work Thursday anyway, so that's two days off," says Coral kindly. "Don't try and do any uni work, either. Just rest."

At that moment, the doorbell rings. It is Heidi.

"I was just passing on my way to hockey practice. Are you okay?"

"Lily hasn't had an easy day," explains Coral."

"I'm not having any easy days right now," adds Lily, with a watery smile. Heidi sizes her up.

"You know, hard as it is to believe given that I'm a hardened Yorkshire woman, I had a terrible time in first year, when I was away from home for the first time, and Gerard left me, and I failed the first semester by misreading a deadline date. I never told any of you because I didn't know you that well yet, but I went to a counsellor, and she really helped me." Heidi pulls out her wallet. "She helped me look at thing differently, and put my problems into perspective. Helped me to see what things are important. I kept her card – well, not on purpose, but I never clean out my wallet – or lose it."

She smirks playfully at Coral, who once lost nine in a term. Mercifully, four of them were empty.

"Okay, I'll give her a call," says Lily. "I'd already decided it's not fair to be moping around like this, bringing everybody down." She waves away Heidi and Tonia's protests that she's doing nothing of the sort. "Thanks, Heidi. Have fun at hockey."

The name on the card in Lily's hand is Maureen Collins. Lily calls her while Coral makes coffee.

"I can see you tomorrow at three," says Maureen. She is quite posh, and sounds very no-nonsense and businesslike. "My fee is thirty pounds per hour." Normal, by all accounts, and Lily's parents will undoubtedly help her to pay for something so important. "See you at three tomorrow." The line does dead.

"Cor, she sounded a bit scary," says Lily cheerfully as Coral enters the room. She feels better for having put the wheels in motion to do something about her problems. "No wonder Heidi liked her."

* * *

"Do you work?" says Maureen.

"Yes. I work at Hope's."

"How many sick days have you had in the past two months?"

How does she know? "Six."

"How many relate to your current emotional state?"

"Two."

"From now on, you go to work," says Maureen firmly. "You will never get better if you hide from the world, not to mention your increased responsibilities." Lily feels a bit uncomfortable with Maureen's chiding tone, but has decided to trust the professional judgement. After all, the way Lily is living now isn't working. Plus, Lily herself is polite and twee to a fault. Everyone else is rude by comparison.

"Do you accept that all your current problems are self-inflicted?" Maureen continues.

"Yes, to a point."

"What do you mean?"

"It takes two to tango," says Lily firmly. "Jacek didn't have a condom either, and he could have said no. Plus, he shouldn't have come straight from Gabriela to me. He should have given himself some time to think. I've told him that."

"And does he accept his share of the responsibility?" probes Maureen.

"Yes, he does."

"Good. So now you need to work on not shirking yours," says Maureen.

"That's why I'm here. I'm physically trying to do everything I have to do. I'm just too tired," points out Lily.

"How many hours of sleep are you getting per night?"

"About ten, and then I have to sleep in the afternoon."

"Cut it down to eight," advises Maureen, "and if you feel the urge to sleep in the afternoon, go for a walk instead. Inertia breeds inertia."

Maureen wants to see Lily the very next day. "I expect to find that you are implementing everything we have agreed upon, and see me whenever I ask you to." She hands Lily a contract saying just that, and Lily signs on the dotted line.

The next day, Lily tries to get up after eight hours' sleep, but is battling to stay awake, and her limbs don't want to move.

"Coral? CORAL!"

Coral appears at the door, bleary-eyed. "What?"

"I'm so sorry to wake you," says Lily sheepishly. "Could you please physically drag me out of my bed, and then you can go back to yours?"

"Why don't you just go back to sleep if you need to?"

"Because Maureen expects to hear at 3pm today that I have done everything she asked me to do yesterday," explains Lily.

Coral's eyebrows arch a little. "She sounds a bit of a dragon! And can you afford thirty quid a day?"

"She is a bit scary," Lily concedes, "but I want to give her a chance. My way of dealing with things wasn't getting me anywhere, and if spending a bit of money now means I can keep going to work and save more money for when the baby's here, so be it. I can't only think about myself anymore."

"You never only thought about yourself, Lily," says Coral warmly as she obediently pulls Lily out of bed.

Lily tries to study, and manages to finish researching for an essay despite her poor concentration. She then goes for a walk instead of going for a nap, which is quite enjoyable, but when she gets home, she knows she can't sit down, or she'll go to sleep. She makes four sandwiches, hands two to Coral, then eats the other two while standing up in the kitchen. Then she cleans and tidies the flat until it is time to go and see Maureen, who is unimpressed by Lily's efforts.

"You're relying on your friends," she says. "Need I remind you that when you finish university you will need to fight this depression alone, so you need to prepare for it."

On balance, Lily thinks that by getting a job – rather than pleading for handouts from Mum and Dad once her student loan is past its adequacy – she has demonstrated her ability to stand on her own two feet. However, it would be nice if she were able to get out of bed without assistance. “Okay, I’ll try harder.”

“How will you try harder?”

Lily thinks back to that morning, and her mind goes blank. What could have counteracted that state of lethargy? “Actually, I’ve no idea. Do you have any pointers?”

“Think about this,” says Maureen. “Your friend is in bed, having a lie-in – which she is entitled to do, as a normal person who isn’t in need special need of structure and routine. Suddenly, she gets a call from her housemate – who has nothing wrong with her legs – asking to be helped out of bed. How does she feel?”

“Most people wouldn’t be very happy, but Coral and I have been best friends for three years, and she knows all about what’s happened. She doesn’t mind.”

Maureen looks hard into Lily’s eyes. “She might not now, but trust me, she will mind very soon. Three years’ friendship down the drain because you couldn’t motivate yourself to get out of bed. How does that sound?”

Lily remembers how everyone in Ryde Secondary School, except her, once stopped speaking to a girl called Mavis, because all she ever did was complain about her life and ask to copy people’s homework. It turned out that both she and her mother were on medication for clinical anxiety and depression – probably hereditary, but triggered by the death of Mavis’ grandfather. She finally understands how Mavis couldn’t concentrate well enough to do her homework. “Okay, I know what you mean. I’ll remember that.”

“What have you eaten today?” asks Maureen. Lily is still getting used to the abruptness of her subject changes.

“Erm… a bowl of cereal, some carrot and cucumber sticks, and a peanut butter sandwich.”

“Don’t eat peanuts, or the baby will be allergic,” orders Maureen. “I take it you haven’t read the latest health advice on pregnancy?”

"I did look at NHS Direct, but I didn't see anything about peanuts on their website. I'm doing all the stuff it says; I've never smoked, I'm not drinking, and I'm avoiding unpasteurised cheeses. I'm taking folic acid."

"Check the additives on your cereal box, also," says Maureen. "If it's got any artificial colours or flavourings, get rid of it. See you at three on Monday."

12

"Did you ever tell Maureen to…"

"Stick it up her arse? Yes, I did," admits Heidi. "It was when she told me I had an addictive personality and should therefore never drink again. It was ridiculous, I admit – just because I got off my face the night Mike left me doesn't make me an addict. But when I told her off, she turned round and said, 'Do you know, I think you're all better, my dear'. And she was right! I think she just pisses you off until your survival instinct has no choice but to kick in."

"I'm not sure I'm going to get any better by being pissed off by someone," says Lily. "I'm quite different from you, Heidi."

"Well, stick it out for a bit longer. You might be surprised, and if not, you can just stop turning up. What's the worst that can happen?"

* * *

The following Monday:

"How often do you drink?"

"Three times a week."

"How much, each time?"

"Two pints on Tuesday and Wednesday. Maybe four on Saturday, but I don't like being drunk, so rarely more than that."

"You're not drunk after four pints?"

"Probably a bit, but I can walk in a straight line and not be sick," says Lily, feeling as silly as she sounds. Maureen makes her feel about eleven years old.

"That implies that you have built up a tolerance, my dear," warns Maureen. "You will lose it while you are pregnant. Please do not attempt to build it up again afterwards." *Perhaps she's anti-drinking, muses Lily. Perhaps someone in her family is an alcoholic.* It has always been difficult to make Lily very drunk, and she's not really any more tolerant to four pints now than when she was sixteen. She doesn't see it as a point worth arguing, though. It won't be relevant for seven and a half months, for starters.

"How is the studying going?" asks Maureen.

"Still trying hard. I can't sit down for too long or else I fall asleep, but I did get all my assignments that are due in two weeks' time done. I'm ahead of schedule, like I wanted to be."

"Finding the energy to study is only going to get harder throughout your pregnancy," observes Maureen. "Do you know what a lectern is?" Lily shakes her head.

"One of those podiums that the lecturer speaks from at your university. Please invest in one, or ask to use lecture halls. Study standing up while you still can."

Wednesday:
"How is your relationship with Jacek?"

"We're fine. We talk at work. It's like old times."

"It is *not* like old times," says Maureen stiffly. "How do you think Gabriela feels, seeing you two having fun together – seeing how much her boyfriend adores the competition?"

Lily tries to imagine how she would feel in Gabriela's position. "Okay, not nice," she concedes, although part of her is convinced that Gabriela knows she's won, and that winning Jacek surely makes one happy at all times.

"Keep your relationship civil at work. Meet outside work only for practical reasons that wholly relate to the child. Friendships in such circumstances is only possible with the mother's permission – and would you dare to ask her permission?" Maureen takes in Lily's saddened expression. "I didn't think so."

Friday:
"What is that?"

"A Starbucks coffee cup," replies Lily.

"What is in it?"

"Coffee," says Lily straightforwardly. She can't quite bring herself to do sarcasm with Maureen.

"Do not drink coffee while you are pregnant. Avoid stimulants in general. Think of the multiplied effect they have on your baby."

All at once, Lily's life has become a treadmill. She drags herself out of bed in the morning by chanting, "Coral will hate me if I don't get up. Coral will hate me if I don't get up. Coral will hate me. Coral *will* hate me."

Breakfasting on plain Shredded Wheat, because everything else seems to have bad bits in it, she goes to uni for a lecture, and then writes some of her dissertation whilst standing at the lectern afterwards. She has already submitted her first two assignments for formative feedback; she gets an email from one lecturer saying, "V. good, no need to resubmit, but not detecting your usual bouncy style – are you okay?"

No, I'm not, admits Lily to herself. Then she switches to, But I will be, if I can get rid of all my selfish moping around and high demands on others. A motivational statement she worked out with Maureen during one of their sessions.

When Lily goes to work, she says hi to everyone, then seeks out all the one person jobs, or says, "I'll come with you," as soon as Lynn or Janet volunteers for a task. She can't work with Jacek and not be herself with him, and now that she has realised the negative impact of being herself with him… Well.

Jacek is upset by this turn of events. Has he done something to hurt Lily? Said something flippant that affected her more than it previously would have done, because of her pregnancy hormones?

Has Gabriela told her to stay away?

He feels unable to ask Gabriela whether or not she has done that, because even if the answer is no, his question might prompt her to think that telling Lily to stay away is a good idea. Because nobody manages to ask Gabriela what she thinks, the fact that she is totally cool with the two of them having normal conversation at work is not discovered – but this fact remains. *After all, Jacek chose me, right?*, thinks Gabriela. She even kind of likes Lily, and definitely feels sorry for her. She can't help realising that her own inadequacy led Jacek to do something silly, which has messed things up for all three of them.

Food is another comfort that has been denied Lily. At least half of her former diet is either now either bad for the baby, or too expensive. At first, it was fun – being on a health kick, but, if anything, being allowed to eat a bit more than usual, as long as it's good for you. However, there is only so much one can take of grilled chicken and steamed vegetables and Shredded Wheat and baked potatoes before one is left craving the life-giving salve of Mr Cadbury. The trouble is, every time Lily comes close to delving into Coral's chocolate stash, all she can hear is Maureen's voice saying, "Your child will almost certainly choose clogged arteries and Type 2 diabetes for itself. Give it the best possible start in life by not making the wrong choice for it."

Lily has also become acutely aware of the effect of her presence on her friends. If she goes to the pub with them, they all want to buy her dinner, or drink less in sympathy. Therefore, in the interests of autarky, she has stopped going. If she is mopey and moody around the house, Coral is likely to feel the need to be sympathetic, so Lily has resolved never to be still, never to give her feelings the chance to breathe. She'll have to rest once she has a bump, after all, and there are things to do before that happens.

She cannot bring herself to admit that the practices that are supposed to be helping her are making her feel tired, lonely, hungry and unhappy. The only emotion Lily allows herself to feel, even to indulge in, is missing Jacek. She knows she would feel that one even if she were sane.

On Tuesday the 10th of February 2012 – two months precisely after the date of Lily's ill-fated dalliance with the love of her life – things begin normally enough. Lily goes to work, and says, "Hi – your team suck – bye," to Jacek, before refilling the World Foods aisle on her own. It's never a job that brings Lily much happiness. Every packet of Polish soup granules nearly makes her cry.

Something is not right that day. If Lily were a volcano or a fault-line, observant geologists would consider evacuating the surrounding area. Pushing her emotions down has not been the solution Lily hoped for, but she refuses to realise this as she goes from work to uni, and puts the emergent final chapter of her dissertation on a lectern.

Ten minutes later, she is still standing there, not having written a word. She has been thinking about how much she would love things to be back to normal with Jacek. To tell everyone that he waved his Polish sausage at her when, in fact, he was innocently filling the World Foods fridge with kielbasa. To put his Man United scarf in the bin, expecting the same rough justice to be dished out to her Arsenal hat. *I wish I'd never slept with him.*

Don't say that, you cow, you don't meant it! replies an older part of Lily.

Yes, I do. The pleasure was not worth it. No pleasure ever is. I've given myself a life sentence of misery, just for one lousy shag.

The fact that there were actually three terrific shags is irrelevant. She can't enjoy the memories anymore. The way she has had to live, since then, has tainted them forever.

She tries to write again. Nothing. Blank. She hears something drop onto her notes. They are wet. She looks to the ceiling, expecting to see a hole in the roof, but the ceiling appears blurry; the only hole is in her heart. Desperate, Lily rings Maureen and asks to meet her at one thirty, instead of three.

"You can't just mess me around like this, you know," says Maureen as Lily arrives, "but as you don't make a habit of it, I'm assuming there's a good reason."

"I apologise, but I'm cracking up."

"How so?"

Lily explains about her day so far; how she reached a point at which she couldn't not cry, couldn't just get on with her work.

"And it was triggered by the realisation that you are repentant of that episode of your life?"

"Yes. I really, really don't want it to have happened now. The only good thing in my life right now was that good memory, and now it's a bad one. I don't know what to do."

"Well, my dear," – to Lily's astonishment, Maureen is smiling delightedly – "I don't think you need me anymore! The one chink of selfishness that was preventing you from moving on with your life is gone."

"But… but I need something! I can't just live in total misery!"

"Let me be perfectly clear. You have messed up your life; therefore there is nothing in it to bring you happiness. Your only chance of happiness is to get your head down, and wait for the time when you will find pleasure and joy in motherhood. Now that you realise that, and have accepted that you are the only one who can take care of yourself, you no longer need my advice. Do you see?"

Lily can't believe what she is hearing. "I came here to see if counselling could make me feel better, but you intended for me to lose all hope?"

"All your false, selfish, girlish hope? Be grateful that it is gone. You will be a far better mother without it."

Lily shoves thirty pounds at Maureen, says, "Well – thanks for everything", and runs out into the street.

Tears are flowing unstoppably down her face now. In an instant, all her defences have collapsed. She needs a hug from a friend. She needs someone to tell her that Maureen is mental. She accepts that everything Maureen has said is a version of the truth. She hopes that it is a skewed, faulty version, but has lost the confidence to make that conclusion for herself. Is the lot of a single mother really to be miserable? she wonders. Is a life without chocolate, beer, friends, love – is it my punishment from God?

She phones Coral. "I need to see you, like, right now."

"Oh, Lils, I'm at my parents'! Don't you remember? My Tuesday class got cancelled, so I went home after Monday's! We'll talk when I get back tomorrow night, yeah?"

Lily phones Tonia's mobile. Heidi's mobile. Their landline. All her parents' numbers. Nothing. Of course, it makes sense for everyone to be busy on a Tuesday afternoon on February. It is just the worst cosmic timing imaginable.

Seeing Hope's, Lily turns towards the entrance, pinning all her hopes on something nice to eat. Her breath is coming in huge gulps, yet none of the air seems to be getting to her lungs

"Are you all right, love?" asks an old man, dragging an uninterested Yorkshire terrier over to her.

"No. But there's nothing you can do. Sorry if I upset you. I'm just going… going to…"

All of a sudden, faintness comes over her. Her head is so light that she must sit down. Here, next to Hope's post box, is fine. She has an awful headache, she realises. Maybe there is some paracetamol in her bag…

With her hand halfway into the bag, darkness falls, and her head cracks hard against the pavement.

Jacek has been allowed to leave work early, because David Hope is trying to save wages. He walks out of the entrance to find a circle of concerned pedestrians, and one unconcerned dog, around a body that has been placed in the recovery position. A body clad in a familiar-looking orange coat, Hope's trousers, and an Arsenal hat…

He runs over. "Can I get through? I'm a friend."

Lily's face is a terrible ivory, tinged with green. There is a small amount of blood at the back of her head.

"I've called an ambulance," says the old man with the dog, gently. "They said ten minutes."

"I think she's bleeding from her leg," calls a woman from the far end of Lily's body. "How do you stop bleeding? Does anyone know First Aid?" Her own knowledge begins and ends with the aforementioned recovery position.

"I do," says Jacek, pulling out two pocket handkerchiefs and springing lightly from one end of Lily's body to the other. He realises that he hasn't quite put his feelings for Lily to bed. That, regardless of her being the mother of his future child, he would give anything for her to be okay.

That she isn't bleeding from her leg.

A great howl escapes him, and a few of the nearest onlookers understand; a young woman, a tiny bump showing under her fashionable top, bends down to Jacek.

"This might not be the end. I had a scare. Tell the ambulance men, as soon as they come, that she might miscarry… Here they are now. I'll tell them. You hold her hand."

He does so, and kneels beside her and kisses her cheek for good measure. It must surely be his fond imagination that this is when she begins to stir. He could have been holding her hand, and watching her anxiously, for hours. All the clocks in the world seem to have stopped, and the ambulance men and woman, bearing a stretcher, may as well be running in slow motion, like the lifeguards on Baywatch.

"Argh, Jacek…" Lily whispers, as an ambulance man moves in to inspect her while his female colleague listens to the other young, pregnant woman. "What's happening? It hurts…"

"Where does it hurt?"

"My head. And my tummy. Like the worst period pain ever. What happened?"

Jacek tries, vainly, to fight back tears. "I don't know, he says gently. What do you remember?"

"Trying to get to Hope's for a chocolate bar."

"That's my girl." He manages a small smile.

"Don't cry, Jacek," she says anxiously, as she is hauled onto a stretcher and sees his face clearly. "I'm going to be fine."

The ambulance woman bends to Lily's level. "What's your name and age?"

"Lily McGoldrick, 21. You probably need to know that I'm pregnant."

"Right. Lily, we think your body might be trying to miscarry, but we're going to get you to hospital, and do everything we can to prevent it. Are you feeling any abdominal pain?"

"Yes, lots."

"How far gone are you?"

"Two months precisely." Then, in spite of the gravity of the situation, she blushes crimson. Jacek doesn't need to know that she thinks of the 10th of December 2011 every day. Used to, anyway. Suddenly, she remembers why she was so upset.

"Jacek, I started to think I wished I'd never slept with you, and my counsellor said this was good, and that I shouldn't be allowed to be happy until I have the baby! And I felt horrible, so I tried to ring everybody but they were all out, and then I was breathing so hard, but I couldn't breathe, and my head hurt so bad…" Then, she is violently sick.

Jacek didn't hear or understand a word. It was too fast, and his brain is too fried. He knows it was serious, and he knows what he has to do. He lifts her hand to his lips, and gives it a tender, warm kiss.

"Whatever you just said," he says, looking straight into her green eyes, "I will listen later. Whatever happens, I will forgive any bad thing you have done, and help you. Now, relax."

It seems like an impossible command, but Lily never heard of any medical condition getting better by the patient worrying about it, and so decides to try.

She says quietly, "Thank you, Jacek… Oh God, please keep my baby safe, or gather her to eternal peace with You." Then, she closes her eyes.

She opens them an hour later in a hospital bed. She knows, from Jacek's swollen, tear-stained face and Gabriela's equally pained one behind him, that all is lost. Her soft, tragic moan attracts the attention of her visitors, and the hospital staff.

"Lily," says a nurse gently, "I am so, so sorry. We did all we could, but we couldn't save your baby."

13

Lily gets through the next few hours, sobbing her heart out, only because of Jacek and Gabriela, holding a hand each, stroking her hair and weeping with her. This is the first that Lily knows of Gabriela's absolute forgiveness and acceptance of her. She realises that if she had known before, she would have had the comfort of Jacek's friendship, and she might still be pregnant… Her resultant, feral, terrible howl breaks Jacek's heart.

Eventually, Lily realises that she must explain to Jacek what happened.

"Gabriela, please can I talk to your boyfriend alone? You can watch through the door."

"Don't worry, I'll get each of us a coffee." Gabriela smiles, and leaves at once.

Lily tells Jacek everything she tried to babble at him previously, plus much more. It is hard to maintain the courage, for Jacek's expression becomes increasingly thunderous. *What happened to his promise to forgive me everything?* Lily wonders. *Ah well, I suppose he has a right to be angry for a time. I just hope he can forgive me later on.*

Jacek, of course, is not remotely mad at Lily. "Your counsellor told you not to be friends with me?" he asks her, still looking volcanic.

"I shouldn't have listened, should I?" asks Lily sadly, tearing up again. "I should have told her to pee off, like Heidi said she did… but I don't think it would have worked. She wanted something else from me. She openly admitted that she wanted me to feel hopeless. She said that, because of what I'd done, there was nothing left in my life to make me happy, so I should stop trying to be."

Jacek's face darkens some more. "I want to know the name and address of this woman. She must not be allowed to work again."

He has never relinquished Lily's hand, not since she was wheeled onto the ward after the doctors and nurses gave up trying to prevent her miscarriage. He squeezes it hard now, stroking along her two longest fingers.

"I said I would forgive you, but I can't." Her face seizes with alarm, and she starts to babble. "Jacek, I'm so sorry – I'll not trouble you again…"

He silences her with a finger to her lips. "I cannot forgive you, because there is nothing to forgive. You have not done anything wrong. You went to somebody for help, because you cared about me and our baby, and she hurt you."

Lily is relieved, grateful and thankful beyond words. All she can manage to say is, "Well, if you're sure… Thank you."

When Gabriela returns, Lily thanks her also. "There was no need for you to stay here, but you did, because you're a wonderful person," Lily says softly. "I'll never be able to repay you, or thank you enough. Either of you."

At that moment, a nurse arrives. "Lily, we're going to keep you in overnight for observation. With your permission, we'd also like you to speak to one of our psychiatric doctors or nurses in the morning. Also, I'm afraid you two will have to leave now," she says to Jacek and Gabriela.

"I'll pick you up tomorrow," Jacek promises. Both he and Gabriela hug Lily, and then they leave, holding hands. Lily feels a strangely unfamiliar heartache at the sight. It is infinitely more pleasant than the grief that feels like it will never end.

* * *

Dr. Mark Kelly is in his mid-thirties, dark-haired, pale-skinned and very friendly and approachable. Lily knows, instinctively, that she can trust him.

"Sometimes, the counsellor or psychiatrist just fits the patient. Other times, they just don't," explains Mark, when Lily has finished her story. "Let's start with what you probably want to know most – and I'm afraid I can't answer conclusively. The best I can do is; we don't know why you miscarried. It could have been the knock on your head; could have been your blood pressure, which was high; could have been your blood sugar, which was low; or it could simply never have been a viable child. Early miscarriages are common," he explains gently. "Ten to twenty percent of pregnancies end in miscarriage, and eighty per cent of these are within the first twelve weeks. How many calories per day do you think you have been eating?"

"Well, I eat quite a lot and very often, but all healthy stuff," says Lily. "I've never counted calories. Just lately, I've been having Shredded Wheat, carrot and cucumber sticks, wholemeal bread, chicken... Maureen warned me off quite a lot of foods, but I made sure I still ate a high volume of food."

"In that case, Lily," says Mark, with utmost sincerity, "I can categorically state that your miscarriage was not your fault. For some reason, your body has been having trouble processing food, hence the low blood sugar, but as you have been eating properly and there were no toxins in your system, I don't think there was any contributory factor on your part."

Lily's entire body slumps forward with relief.

"We'll take a second blood test from you, just before you leave, to make sure you don't have diabetes, but there are many causes of hypoglycaemia.

"Now," Mark continues, "I think this is going to be difficult for you to take in, because it must be hard to have two supposed experts telling you different things. It is my opinion that a lot of what you were told by your counsellor was either not right for you, or not right per se. Did she ever give you a personality test to take?"

"No. She seemed quite perceptive, though. She always seemed to ask a question about something I had a problem with, somehow."

"That is quite easy, for a counsellor," says Mark. "She will have seen a lot of people with symptoms of mild to moderate depression. From what you told me, she missed the mark with some of her suggestions, too. If she had got you to take a personality test, she would have been able to deal with you more appropriately. I can tell, just from this brief interview, that you are not the sort of person who is motivated by harsh criticism. Your reaction is more likely to be, 'Okay, so I'm a bad person', rather than, 'I'm going to prove you wrong'. Now, how would you like to talk through a few of the thoughts and fears that caused you to become depressed?"

Lily does. It's a long conversation, and she is determined to hold some of Dr Kelly's responses in her head, and her heart, for a long time.

"Eighty percent of British people don't use a condom the first time they have sex. We doctors do like to ram the point home about contraception, but that doesn't mean that people who get pregnant deserve to live in misery. I think you can count yourself unlucky, without the need for self-flagellation.

"You are very young, and very much in love. I can honestly say that as a third-year medical student, I would not have handled a boy/girl situation as maturely and rationally as you have. I think this is the reason Gabriela likes you so much.

"The advice to avoid burdening your friends is some of the worst I've ever heard. I think you have the common sense to know when you have the right to ask for help, and how much whinging is too much. Believe me when I say that your friends have probably been more worried about you because you've kept yourself to yourself, than they would have been if you'd kept up your social life. They wouldn't have minded you being a bit grumpy occasionally.

"A chocolate bar won't kill you and wouldn't have harmed your baby, unlike a lot of bad habits I could name. Do you mind if I just nip out for a fag? I'll be back in a minute."

Lily remembers being about seven and picking up one of her brother's magazines. A celebrity had- very publicly- been attending psychotherapy sessions, and in this interview he had said, 'Counselling's like having a sauna; you come out feeling fresh.' She never understood that remark until now. She doesn't feel right as rain, just a heck of a lot better.

"Now," says Mark, "I can tell you that you've probably not seen the last of feeling miserable. How about we go through some positive strategies that will help you, bit by bit, to feel better?" Lily takes notes, and will late type these notes up into a plan of action, which will read thus:

'Sleeping all day probably isn't the best idea, but be honest about how much sleep you need. Getting up when your housemate does is fine. Going for a walk every day is a good idea, and if you need a nap afterwards, that's fine, too. Try and set a time for it. Having a friend come and drag you out of bed is extremely effective, and completely harmless.

Eating healthily is good, but eating comfort food occasionally isn't necessarily bad. Watch out for unhealthy patterns, like not eating for long periods, binge eating, being unable to stop eating, and eating so quickly that you're not really tasting anything, but still wanting more after each mouthful.

If you need more time to do an assignment, lecturers should be sympathetic to the reasons why. To aid concentration, take a break as soon as you realise you're not doing anything – a short walk around the garden is effective, as is a cup of tea and a biscuit.

Jacek and Gabriela seem like incredible people who like you, so don't hide away from them. Why create awkwardness when it isn't there?

Never eat shredded wheat.'

Lily thanks Dr Kelly profusely as she prepares to leave hospital.

"I thought that woman wasn't right for me, but then I was miserable anyway, so I thought seeing her must have been better than doing nothing," Lily admits.

"Don't mention it. Unfortunately, there are a lot of people out there charging for the wrong kind of advice. If you feel the need to talk to someone like that again, there are good people out there. Try asking your GP for details, or go through Mind or Sane, the mental health charities. People at your church probably know some good Christian counsellors, too, if you think that would be helpful. Take care of yourself, Lily. In the nicest possible way, I hope I'll never see you again."

Jacek arrives to collect Lily, as promised, right on time, being a typically punctual Pole. Lily is aware that he can't be feeling all that great himself.

"Do you need someone to talk to?" Lily asks Jacek, squeezing his arm as they walk to his car.

"I spoke to Dr Kelly yesterday. He was just clocking on as Gabriela and I left your room. Your nurse realised that I wasn't coping as well as I – what do I mean?" His English fails him.

"You weren't really as strong as you felt you had to be for me," Lily guesses perfectly.

"Dr Kelly is a good man," says Jacek. "I wish you had met him before."

They spend the car journey home in comradely, companionable silence. Lily's heart still beats faster every time he is within thirty feet of her. He is a good nerve tonic or, at the very least, a much tastier alternative to Berocca.

At her flat, he insists on coming in. Still no Coral.

"Coffee?" Lily asks. He takes the kettle from her.

"Sit down, and don't play with electrical… things."

"Appliances."

"Whatever. You lost some blood. I don't want you passing out, with boiling water everywhere," he says firmly.

Once the switch is flicked, his tone changes as he wanders over to Lily, and says gently, "Do you want to call your mum now?"

She nods, and he rests his hands on her shoulders as she finds her phone and speed-dials her mother.

"Hello, Lily darling. I called last night, but your phone was off."

"Mum, I have some bad news. I lost the baby."

She inevitably dissolves into sobs as she says the word, 'baby'. Jacek hugs her close, pulling her head against his chest. His heartbeat is faster and more jittery than when she lay on his chest after their lovemaking. She finds his hand, giving it a reassuring squeeze.

"Oh, sweetheart, I'm so sorry," says Lily's mum, also in tears. "Are you okay?"

"I'll be okay," hiccoughs Lily.

"Does Jacek know?"

"Yes. He's here now, being my hero." She laughs giddily. "I must let him go soon, so Gabi can kiss him better."

She wants Jacek to be kissed better, no matter who by. The thought of it... Why, it touches that blissful spot in her chest! It shall hereby renamed the 'Jacek is happy so I'm happy' spot. *Wow,* Lily thinks – and there's a sudden lightning bolt of happiness to be found in the thought – *I've grown up a little.*

"I'll tell your father," says Lily's mum gently. "Dan didn't know you were pregnant. Can I tell him everything?" Lily and her twenty four-year-old brother are close, but she didn't trust him not to get drunk and congratulate her on her pregnancy on Facebook, where all her school friends' older brothers would see it.

"Yes, please," says Lily. "And I'll come home sometime soon, but only if you promise to be normal. One teary hug when we meet, and that's it. The rest of the time, we'll go for walks, and go bowling, and ride Hilda."

Hilda is Lily's favourite horse at the local stables, where she mucks out in return for riding opportunities.

"Fine by me, and fine if you change your mind and need to cry at any time."

Lily's mum, Lucy, is a saint. Her dad, Michael, is too. Their twenty six year marriage is probably the reason Lily's vision of wedlock is so impossibly perfect.

Lily and her mum ring off, and Lily hugs her preferred husband of choice round the middle, longing to comfort him. Jacek's emotional bruises are soothed just a little by her touch. *It's sad, really,* thinks Jacek. *It's like I'm a machine, and Lily and Gabriela both know what lots of the buttons do. I wish just one person had the manual.*

He makes coffee, and he and Lily sit in silence for a while, holding hands. It is just what they both need, a beautiful absence of both stimulation and loneliness.

Lily breaks the silence. "Get yourself home."

"You want me to go?"

"Yes, because you need to hug and kiss Gabriela and tell her what an angel she's been and how much you love her, and then she's going to reciprocate."

She wishes she could text Gabriela some instructions, without being too patronising. She's sure Gabi knows to hug and kiss him, but whether her imagination stretches as far as Lily's does when it comes to making a man feel better... Doubtful. Nobody's does, probably.

Jacek knows she is right, although he feels drained of the energy to make the journey. "Call Sue and tell her what happened. I'll call you tomorrow."

They hug and kiss each other on the cheek, and then he is gone. Lily abruptly feels like he has left her again, and howls. So much for having grown up- although it still feels quite good to think of Gabi kissing him better. She calls Sue, who falls over herself to provide sympathy, and offers to come over.

"Thanks but no thanks, Sue. I think I need to take a nap. Hospital is like a train journey. It's the most tiring doing nothing you could possibly imagine."

"Okay. Don't worry about this week. I'll put you down as on compassionate leave. Call me on Saturday if you don't think you can manage Monday."

When Sue gets off the phone, she realises Sally is hovering. The two sisters get on reasonably well, in spite of Sally's epic rudeness.

"What's wrong?" asks Sue.

"Did she lose her baby?"

"How did you know she was pregnant?"

"I'm not blind. I'm just as observant as you are. I've just never considered it for a career. Did she?"

"Yes, she did, and it's..."

"Confidential. I know. Shame, I kind of like young Lily. Why do the good girls always waste their emotions on bloody oversexed stallions who don't know what side their bread's buttered?"

"I think Jacek's bread is buttered in all directions," muses Sue. "It can't be easy for him, or Gabi, or any of his other admirers."

As the pair get back to work, Sue observes that this is the first time Sally has openly expressed admiration for any of her Hope's colleagues. There must be something in the water, or maybe an impending recall on Sally's favourite Scotch eggs, due to the accidental inclusion of a powerful opiate. Now *that* would make the local TV news…

Coral pushes through the door at seven-thirty to find Lily huddled under a blanket on the sofa, dead to the world.

"Lils?" She pushes her shoulder, knowing that Lily was trying not to nap.

Lily yawns, sees Coral, then promptly bursts into tears. "I lost it, Coral. I had a miscarriage."

"Oh, shit. Shit, shit, shit!" Is that what you were trying to tell me when you phoned?"

"No. I phoned because I was cracking up. Then I cracked my head on a post box, and that could have caused it; or two other medical problems I didn't know about…"

Lily's words dissolve into fresh tears. Coral pulls her into a sitting position, then sits beside her and hugs her as tight as she can.

"I'm sorry, Lils, so sorry."

"'S nobody's fault. Will you stay here with me for a while?"

The girls huddle together under Lily's blanket until morning, sleeping, weeping and saying nothing.

Not far away, Gabriela snuggles into Jacek's chest, her warmth taking the edge off his pain and rage. Jacek and Lily take comfort in other people as they each feel their own personal loss, and worry about each other.

The next day, Lily and Coral go round to Tonia and Heidi's, just as they did a month before, but with much more difficult news. Heidi is distraught.

"Oh my, I told you to go and see that terrible woman! Lily, you have no idea how sorry I am."

Lily holds her hands. "It's not your fault at all. You did your best to help."

"I can't believe she told you your friends basically didn't care about you," Tonia sighs. "You won't believe how much we've missed you these last couple of weeks. Don't forget that we always want to see you, even if you need to have a whine and a moan."

When Coral and Heidi go into the kitchen to make dinner, Lily says, "Tonia, before I slept with Jacek I prayed that if God didn't want it to happen, it wouldn't. Do you think He made sure I had a non-viable child to punish me?" The question has been playing on her mind all day.

Tonia gets up from her usual seat and moves to sit next to Lily on the sofa.

"No, I don't believe that," she says softly. "Have you read the book of Job? It's hard to understand, but I think the point of it is that you can be as good as you like, and bad things still might happen to you. Also, the Gospel says that bad things don't happen to people because they're worse sinners than everybody else. Bad things happen to everyone, and everyone's a sinner."

"Why do you think God let me sleep with Jacek, if He knew what would happen, then? To teach me a lesson?"

Tonia puts her head on one side and considers. "You know, I think that if you'd heard God clearly say, 'No', you might have done it anyway, but not enjoyed it. That's happened to me in the past. If my heart's completely set on something, I find it hard to stop, and then I just have a bad experience when I could have had a good one…" She takes Lily's hand. "All I know is that the loving God that we serve wouldn't do something like this to us. Evil comes from the devil, not God. I don't see God's hand in what happened to you. It hasn't made you a better person, has it? It hasn't made you a worse person either, but I think if something comes from God, you see positive change, not a person becoming sick and depressed."

Lily sighs. "I want to believe you, but there's still part of me that will always blame myself for this. I know one thing; I'm definitely not going to sleep with another man until I get married, so if that's what God has been trying to teach me, then He's succeeded."

"Perhaps you could say that *you* are making a decision to make your life purer and grow as a Christian – which makes you good, rather than God horrible," says Tonia sagely.

14

Things gradually return to something approaching normal. Lily visits her mum and dad, and together they manage to have a great family time without too much blubbing. Dan takes Lily to watch Arsenal, where the Gunners very nearly complete an astonishing fight back against AC Milan, racing into a 3-0 lead by half time, but never finding the crucial fourth goal that would have overturned the Italian side's 4-0 victory in the away match three weeks beforehand. Tonia and Simon, still going strong, take Lily to an open mic night at uni and talk her into performing 'Right Here Waiting' on the piano, as she has often previously done at student parties.

She slowly regains confidence, and starts to feel better. There are dark days, when she can't get out of bed and feels like the most evil person on Earth, but as spring comes, they become fewer and further between.

"Never underestimate the weather," says Jacek to Lily at work, noticing the old spring come back into her step on a bright March morning.

He, too, is feeling better; he and Gabriela have even socialised with Lily and her friends once. On this occasion, Lily finally managed to drink a pint. She'd been feeling uncomfortable with drinking – partly because of Maureen's anti-alcohol stance, which had become embedded in her consciousness, and partly because of a nagging sense that drinking was a way of screaming, 'Hallelujah, I'm not pregnant anymore!' She increasingly has peace in not being pregnant anymore; neither the relief of a woman who had been thinking about abortion, nor the grief of one who had been desperate for a child. Just sadness, regret, and peace.

Lily also gets involved in the Mental Health Awareness Week that the Students' Union organises in mid-March. She has already stepped up her political campaigning, looking to eradicate opportunities to sit around and think about what happened, and it feels empowering to try and help other young people to avoid what happened to her.

"Go through your GP or a mental health charity," she advises a young woman who is having trouble sleeping and eating. "If you really feel uncomfortable with what a counsellor is telling you, try and find a different one. Not every counsellor respects your individuality, but a good one should."

"Good advice!" says a man's voice behind Lily.

She turns around to see a young man, applauding her without irony. He is slightly taller than her, with brown hair and rather enticing dark eyes, and is dressed in a sort of universal posh-bloke uniform – green shirt, blue jeans, those brown trainers that a doorman will usually pretend not to see – but the green suits him, and he doesn't look pretentious.

"I'm Amos," he says, extending a hand.

"Lily," she replies. "Interesting name. Are you Jewish?"

"No. A nurse sent a Gideon Bible flying with her impressive behind as she was lifting me off the delivery table, and it fell open on the book of Amos. Mum had thought of about thirty-five suitable names for a girl child, but no boys' names, and she and my dad liked Amos."

Lily giggles. "I have this problem, too. I have no sensible boys' names."

"How do you mean, sensible?" It's four o'clock, and Lily begins to assist the other student volunteers in packing away for the day as she talks.

"Well, I like names that would get the poor child into real trouble at secondary school. Like… Gideon, funnily enough. Or Isaiah, which will be fine if my husband is black. Or Zdzislaw."

"Or *what*?"

"Zdzislaw. It's Polish. The last guy I was involved with was Polish, and I think their names are amazing. I know what I'm going to call my first daughter – Katarzyna."

"Will her friends be able to pronounce it?"

"Well, if her dad is Polish, I'll shorten it to Kasia, like the Poles do. I knew a lovely girl here at uni called Kasia. But if the dad's English, I might just have to stick with plain old Kate."

* * *

Okay, you've got me. Lily's my mum. I think most of you guessed that already, from the fact that I said this was my mum's story really, and I guess the dates add up, too. But you think you know something about me now, don't you? You think you know who my dad is – I mean, that he's English, and therefore, who he isn't? I expect some of you are horribly disappointed, and some of you are quite pleased. Whichever camp you fall into, please, please read the rest of the book.

* * *

Amos and Lily end up exchanging numbers. When he shakes her hand, she looks into his brown eyes and feels a bit fluttery. From whence did this come? she wonders. Is she – gasp! – about to Move On From Jacek, at long last?

"He's in Coral's and my Shakespeare class," says Tonia later.

"Ugh, that means he's delusional, like all the other wannabe Hamlets and history bores who take Shakespeare – present company excepted," interjects Heidi.

"He's a drama student, so probably a wannabe Hamlet," says Lily. "As long as he has no intention of taking me to watch a Shakespeare play, that's fine by me."

"Why do you take English literature, Lily?" asks Coral, shaking her head. "You're not even into English stuff. Or men."

"I'm good at essays, I read books really fast, and I like the contemporary stuff. I just accept that you have to read a load of incomprehensible twaddle that Tory education ministers think is good because it's old, as a sort of down payment on being able to do a degree in something vaguely interesting. And who says I don't like English men? Just because I do like foreign men… The two interests aren't mutually exclusive, you know."

*   *   *

"Lily!"

She turns. "Amos! How goes it?"

She's about to turn into a lecture theatre, and Amos has run up behind her, wearing a St. Pauli football T-shirt over his uniform jeans.

"Oh my! St Pauli! That is SO cool! Best fans in the world – well, them and Livorno. I really want a Livorno shirt, but you can't seem to buy one anywhere."

"I got this one from my brother. He works in Hamburg, in a bank. He could have worked in a bank here, except his degree was in Economics and German, so he thought he'd use it."

"You have an older brother? Mine too. What's yours called?"

"Daniel."

"Mine too! Dan and Dan, like those guys who made that YouTube video about the Daily Mail."

"Haven't seen it, I'm afraid."

Lily's lecturer enters the hall and gives her an 'are you coming in?' look on her way through the door.

"Meet me in the library in two hours, and I'll show you."

Amos laughs so hard when he sees the Daily Mail video that the library security guard comes and warns him about his future conduct.

"Sorry," he whispers. "It won't happen again… That was amazing, Lily!"

"Shall we discuss it over coffee, so he doesn't suspend our borrowing privileges?" suggests Lily.

"Well, I'd actually love a cup of tea…"

"You sound like my mum. Race you to the refectory, Mum, and don't forget your handbag!"

15

Amos and Lily lie on the grass outside his halls of residence. His arm has found its way around her shoulders, and she doesn't mind. How did they get here? Lily has had an interesting day at work, courtesy of Sally Hill.

"Jacek, that shelf is a mess, yet again. Clear off and mess up somewhere else. Gabriela, go and hold his hand."

Ugh. That leaves Lily alone with the local misanthropist. She is surprised, therefore, to hear Sally say, "How's it going, Lily?"

"Oh, the usual. Counting down the days to my pension cheque. It's all right for you clever girls. You'll never be stuck here forever."

"I dunno – look at Hazel. No one can say she didn't get herself educated, or work hard at Nugent and Sweeney, but bam – there's a recession, no firm, no job, and here she is."

"Yes, but I don't think this is the end for her, do you?"

"No. She'll probably end up marrying an ageing but very sexy French vintner, inheriting a chateau, and making its wines the best in the world."

"You have an overactive imagination, my dear," says Sally, condescendingly, but not unkindly.

"You don't need to have one to work here, but it helps."

"Touché."

"So, what did you always want to be, when you were growing up?" ventures Lily.

"I was in the British Olympic ice skating team in 1994. I always thought I'd do that for a living, but then I fell down three flights of stairs and shattered my ankle, and that was the end of that. Then I went to uni, but dropped out."

"You could always do Open University."

"Can't afford it," says Sally simply. "Anyway, I got a decent office job, but dared to say 'no' when the boss's son asked me out, so I was" – she wiggles her fingers – "made redundant. Then Sue got me the job here, and twelve years later, here we are."

"So, a litany of bad luck and misogyny, then."

Sally suddenly turns. "Lily, I know... what happened. Don't worry, nobody told on you. I'm just good at working these things out, like my sister. I suppose I have no right to expect you to listen to me about this, but... when I dropped out of university, it was because I was pregnant."

Lily is beginning to understand Sally a bit better. "So what happened?"

"I lost it at four months. I dropped out because I was due to have the baby during my finals, which were all-or-nothing. I couldn't just repeat my final year – I would have had to start again. The whole academic world was misogynistic, more recently than you'd think. Then, suddenly, I had no baby and no future." Just for a second, she looks as if she might cry. "Then my boyfriend left me – probably a good thing. The very same man who pushed me down those stairs when I was seventeen. Don't worry – he wasn't behind me losing the baby. He just ran off abruptly, having used threats and abuse to make me stay by his side for five years."

"Oh, my word, Sally, I'm so sorry."

"Don't be. It was years ago. Anyway, then that idiot Ben Sawyer asked me out, and I said no straightaway, because he was slow, unintelligent and uninteresting. Personality like Gabriela, and looks like Jim." She barks with laughter. "I never thought it would cost me my career, or that no man would look at me twice for the next twelve years. Even so, were I to do it again, I'd still have said no to Ben, but refused to work at Hope's until the dole office dragged me here, kicking and screaming." She wags her finger at Lily. "I think you and Jacek were carved from the same block, but since he seems to prefer the juvenile airhead, then my only advice is not to turn your nose up at a decent man who you're just a little attracted to."

"So, where's yours, then?" asks Lily gently.

"Ha! I'm thirty six years old. I don't just need Botox; I need a miracle!"

Lily leaves work with a new understanding of Sally, and a little excitement brewing inside her. She is meeting Amos at the university theatre, where the gospel choir is giving a matinee performance for local pensioners. Amos is involved with the choir, and asked Lily to come to his performance. All in all, it is an enjoyable afternoon. Amos has a fantastic bass-baritone voice, and the whole exercise looks like such tremendous fun that Lily kicks herself for joining the Left Society instead (singing rehearsals had clashed with revolution rehearsals when she had first made enquiries, three years previously).

"That was amazing, Amos! You were great," enthuses Lily over a glass of warm white wine afterwards.

"Why, thank you. I do love my singing – anything dramatic, really. I'm hoping to go into to musical theatre after uni – I understudied Marcus Brigstocke in Spamalot at the Mayflower two years ago."

"That's quite an achievement for a nineteen-year-old first year!"

"That's one way of looking at it, the other being that I look like someone's dad."

"And dress like their granddad… For heavens' sake, Amos, I'm kidding!" He had looked rueful. "You are one of those men who could be fifteen or thirty, and you'll look thirty until you're fifty."

Amos has to go back to his hall of residence then to turn off the oven. One of his flatmates had expressed his intention to put a cake on, *then* go for a lecture; "You'll turn it off, Amos mate, won't you?"

Amos asks Lily along. As a matter of fact, the flatmate, Brian, has forgotten to switch the oven on, thus thwarting Amos and Lily's plan to dump it and then go for a pint. This is how they end up lying on the grass outside in the mid-spring sunshine, and Amos tucks his arm around Lily, and she doesn't mind; and when he starts to softly, slowly stroke her arm, she doesn't mind one bit.

Lily's decision not to sleep with someone else until she is married is not just because of her faith, and her doomed pregnancy, but because of a feeling that making love to Jacek has created a bond that cannot be broken. This is fine, because it's Jacek, and the two of them are making a very good job of just being friends, but Lily fears that making random bonds all over the place could make her unstable, like Uranium-235 or something.

Lily tells Amos about all the year's dramas when they eventually get down to the Union for a pint. He's sympathetic, and not scared, as Lily feared he would be. He understands and accepts her decision about sex; he is a virgin.

"I was never really attracted to a woman before you, Lily," he blushes. "I think trying to make it happen was making it harder. My mum will be thrilled to hear that I've got a girlfriend. She sort of thinks that everyone who doesn't settle down has to become a monk, or otherwise they'll live a life of sin."

"Sounds like my friend's mum," says Lily, thinking of Tonia's mum. "Is she a member of a heavy shepherding church?"

"She wouldn't give birth in a room without a Bible in it."

"Figures."

Tonia, as it happens, is the only one of Lily's friends who doesn't seem thrilled with Amos. He meets the girls over several pints in front of the Benfica-Chelsea Champions League quarter-final.

"He is so sweet," smiles Coral after he's gone. "Quite different from Jacek, but they're both lovely."

"He's yin to Jacek's yang," agrees Lily. "I kind of get the feeling that I could love – really love – Amos without running out of adrenaline, or whichever chemical makes you hot and bothered, and, funnily enough, I don't miss that chemical."

"Only 'cos you're getting it from Jacek at work," says Tonia shrewdly.

"Maybe, but I'm just not thinking about Jacek all the time now, and I'm quite enjoying the rest. This is more how I used to feel about boys before I knew there were explosive ones, and there's nothing wrong with it. I know – finding out that there's nothing wrong with it was a surprise to me, too."

"I think you have more in common with Amos," observes Heidi. "You'll be able to have conversations of mutual understanding, not just bickering and play-fighting. Don't get me wrong – Jacek is outrageously hot, and not thick by any means, but you can *so* tell he never went to uni, and I think you'd get sick of that after a while."

"Opposites attract, though, and if Lily and Jacek can be friends without sleeping together, I think their mutual appreciation must be sustainable," argues Tonia.

"Lily, what have you done to Tonia's brain?" giggles Coral. "That's the deepest thing I've ever heard her say."

"Listen, Lily," says Tonia gently, "I don't think Amos is the one for you, but I'm willing to be proved wrong, and I'm going to be nice to him. All I will say is, don't throw yourself in there hook, line and sinker – I think that's a mixed metaphor, but you know what I mean. Tread carefully."

"I'm afraid I don't know how," says Lily regretfully. "I think I agree with that author that said, 'People who are sensible about love are incapable of it'."

It's April. The usual mix of outrageously unseasonal heat, and safe, predictable old rain, arrives. Lily turns her usual shade of golden brown, an instant tan in the first two hours of summer, which will never darken, not even if she backpacks around the Equator. She suspects that this is a sign of strong, youthful skin and the unlikelihood of skin cancer, but she still doesn't like it very much. This is not a view shared by Jacek, who is desperately trying not to stare at her glowing face all day, and wishing Gabriela didn't insist on tanning the salon way – it just isn't the same.

Amos is tanned to a rich bronze, which Lily likes a lot. It is probably why they end up laying on his bed all day one Wednesday, touching each other here and there. It is all fairly innocent at first, because Amos isn't sure of doing anything guilty.

"I'm not asking you to give me your virginity – we've talked about that," says Lily reassuringly. "I just feel good right now, and I'd quite like you to touch me here." She places his palm on the top of her breast, clearly visible above her vest top.

Amos smiles, a more nervous smile than usual. "It feels a bit strange."

"Girls usually have softer skin than boys, especially in the places we usually cover up. Is it good strange, or bad strange?"

"I don't know," he whines, a little snappily.

"Shh, just relax. Don't do anything you don't feel comfortable with." They rest in this position for a while, and eventually Amos finds the courage to graze Lily's nipple with his thumb a few times, given confidence by her sigh of "That… feels… amazing." He manages to touch her in a few other amazing places after that.

"It's interesting that you like to be touched so gently," observes Amos, much later.

"Another difference between boys and girls."

"No. I… went this far with a girl before. I was almost forced into it, but not against my will. She was pushier than you, and I was drunk, and wanted to do stuff with a girl because I thought that's what horny teenagers did. Anyway, she liked it really rough, and I was worried that I was hurting her, but she loved it."

"What happened to her?"

"She's a lesbian." He chuckles. "I think my ineptitude may have turned her."

"I wouldn't be so sure," murmurs Lily, whose current glow has nothing to do with her sun-kissed skin. "Oh, that reminds me. There's a march on the Saturday after next, past the Conservative Club, against these right-wing charities that the Tories are bringing into schools to teach sex education. It's organised by the LGBT Society, but they want all good students to go along in solidarity. Fancy it?"

"Solidarity, eh?" says Amos, with a flicker of an odd smile that Lily can't quite read. "I think you may be addicted to solidarity, my dear. A member of the demonstrating classes." He's referring to her recent flurry of political activity. "Are you sure you were on the right side of that mental health table the other day?"

"I think all those who give good advice on the right side have been on the wrong side at some point," says Lily, thoughtfully. "Without that experience, you probably just end up thinking you can fix people, and judging them." She is thinking of Maureen Collins.

"Well, I quite agree, and I'd love to join you for a spot of solidarity. It's a date."

16

One thing Amos doesn't seem interested in is reciprocation of the good things he does to Lily. After their conversation about solidarity, Lily tries to work her magic on him. It's never failed before, and such is her attention to detail that most men end up gasping things like 'What have you done to me?' while holding their stomachs. (Now, why do men hold their stomachs when enjoying themselves with a lady? I've never understood that.) But Lily's attention seems to leave Amos cold.

Eventually he says, "I don't expect tit for tat, Lily. You relax."

He turns on the TV. Lily isn't unduly worried, though; she assumes he's suffering from stress. She can see the towering pile of scripts and Shakespeare plays on his bedside table, and knows that she's probably the only student in England to have finished her dissertation this early.

The following Wednesday, Lily and Amos go to the Students' Union for a Vicars and Tarts disco. Lily is wearing her tarty dress from the Christmas do. It is with a pang of regret that she pulls it on. The last time she wore this dress, it led to the best few days of her life, followed, eventually, by the worst. If she were superstitious, she'd have burned or buried it; but she's not, so she pairs it with black fishnets and a pair of heels that she can barely walk in. She hopes Amos won't mind having to look up her nose, rather than into her eyes, for a change.

"Wow," he says, when he sees her. He's dressed in one of his standard black shirts, with the addition of a chopped-up Fairy Liquid bottle. "You look amazing! What have I done to deserve the belle of the ball on my arm?"

"The washing up?" she suggests, playfully jabbing his 'dog collar'.

All Lily's friends and all Amos' friends are going to the dance; for most of them, it is a last hurrah before exam revision kicks in. Lily leaves them all stood in a group while she and Maurice, a friend of Amos' from the choir, hit the bar, laden with a two-pound coin each from twenty people.

"Great performance last week in front of the old folks," Lily enthuses, as they wait for four jugs of Sex on the Beach to be prepared.

"Thank you, although I hear you don't think it's as great as arranging freedom for Palestine over cappuccinos on Thursday evenings."

"Oh, Amos has told you all about me, then? Good to know!"

When they return to the group, trying not to spill the pitchers they have in each hand, Amos is chatting excitedly to Justin, a boy from one of Lily's English classes. He's a nice enough lad, but all she really knows about him is that he supports Bristol City and doesn't like Niall Ferguson (his argument with a Tory in an elective History class in first year taught her that).

"Lily! This is Justin, my new best friend! Did you know that he lived in Hamburg for a year and had a season ticket at St. Pauli?" enthuses Amos.

"No! Why didn't you tell me about that when I asked you who you support on the second day of first year?" demands Lily.

"Because I only found out you were a raving Marxist when you backed me up against that Tory later on in the term, and I couldn't very well stop arguing that Britain was not solely responsible for global civilisation in order to talk about football."

"Wow. So how come you don't come to Left Society?"

"Clashes with hockey practice, and while I agree that the workers' struggle is far more important than the struggle to control a little white ball, I'm going to the Olympics this summer, and I'm too selfish to pass up such an opportunity."

"Not selfish. Ambitious."

Lily was just opening her mouth to say that, but Amos said it instead. *Wow, she thinks, we really are similar.*

"They really need to invent a week with two Thursdays," she says, instead. "Everything I want to do at uni is on a Thursday. Plus I don't like giving up Tuesdays or Wednesdays, 'cos those are for football and drinking."

"Lily, come and *daaaaaance*". Heidi drank a bottle of wine before she came out.

"Why not? Coming, Amos?"

"In a minute. Justin has to finish telling me about his gap year in Malawi first."

"Tonia is Malawian," says Lily, and hastily introduces Tonia and Simon to Justin before going to dance rowdily with Heidi and Coral.

Amos never does come to dance. Lily doesn't mind; she's not given to minding little omissions like that, and she's happy that he and Tonia seem to be getting on well, mostly through the medium of crazy mum stories. At the end of the night, just about everyone comes back to Amos' hall for a party, and just about everyone falls asleep on the kitchen table after three rounds of Ring of Fire. Lily, Amos and Justin are soon the last ones standing. They talk animatedly at first, about books, films and politics, and slip into a comfortable silence.

"Lily," says Amos suddenly, "were you expecting to stay the night?"

"Not expecting, but I'd like to, but only if you want me to."

"If you do, would you mind nabbing that sofa in the corner before anyone else does? I'm getting a blinding headache, and I don't think extra warmth will be good for it."

"I see you asking me to sleep on the sofa, and I raise you giving you a fantastic neck massage, and still not minding sleeping on the sofa," drawls Lily, stumbling over to him and starting to knead his muscles.

She works for a while, talking over Amos to Justin about learning massage from library books because her first boyfriend had a multiplicity of football injuries, about their respective dissertations, and about the travelling they're going to do after university. Talking about this subject always induces both excitement and regret in Lily – the peaceful regret she feels when she is reminded that she can only do something because she lost her baby.

Eventually, she laces her hand in Amos' hair, scratching slightly, and says, "Okay, I'm going to sleep now."

"Don't you dare, Liljana," says Amos through a mouthful of his own sleeve – his head has dropped peacefully onto his folded arms. "If you stop playing with my hair, I'll be traumatised for life."

"Liljana! I like that! Would it be too egocentric to name a baby Liljana? Or is that something I can only do if the dad is Croatian or Serbian, rather than Amos Barkley?"

"No, *you're* my Liljana. No more Liljanas."

(He's right, you know. I don't have a sister called Liljana, and it's not my middle name, either. I hope someone in my family calls a girl Katarzyna Liljana one day, though. That's an awesome name!)

The following Sunday, Lily goes swimming with Tonia after they both return from their respective churches.

"So, do you like Amos now?" Lily asks Tonia over a coffee in the canteen afterwards. Lily's dark brown hair is showing more of its natural red highlights because it's slightly wet. Various men look over appreciatively. Lily wishes more of them were looking at Tonia, and wonders why you see loads of white women out with black men, but not many white men out with black women.

"I always liked him, Lils, but I still don't think you have a future together. Just my opinion."

"You want me to wait for Jacek, don't you?"

"Not really, although as the hottest man in the world finds you attractive, I'd consider it. Look, Lily…" She takes Lily's hands and looks earnestly into her green eyes. "I think, pretty soon, you and Amos are going to part on friendly terms. If he tells you why, you might not be surprised, and if he doesn't, I promise to tell you what I think."

"Tonia, what are you talking about?"

"I don't want to say, in case I'm wrong. All I can say is, if you're still together in a few months, I'll happily eat my words."

Lily goes home and finds Coral emptying the cupboards of spaghetti Bolognese ingredients, with the radio on. People on the radio are talking earnestly about HIV and condoms.

"Sounds a bit heavy for Sunday evening. Be glad I didn't bring Tonia home with me. She'd have turned anything serious off," points out Lily. "What is it?"

"What's Your Problem?"

"I'm sorry – did I offend you?"

"No, sorry, it's a phone in called 'What's Your Problem?'. Not like those trashy TV agony shows where they make pathetic single parents feel even worse than they already did, but a sympathetic one. I quite enjoy finding out what to do in case of fire… I mean, in case of all manner of personal problems."

She's standing next to the landlord's fire prevention sign. The girls fall silent and listen to other people's problems – racist parents, sexist parents, alcoholic parents. It doesn't take a university education to work out that this week's programme is entitled 'Problem Parents'.

"Our next caller wishes to remain anonymous, so in our usual style, we'll give him the first name that comes into our heads… Derek. Good evening, Derek. What's your problem?"

"I'm gay, and my parents are fundamentalist Christians," says a voice that sounds high and odd – probably higher than usual through nerves.

"Poor sod," observes Coral as she plunges some spaghetti into boiling water. The next few words are obscured by the pan boiling over.

"…try to get a girlfriend and see if I can change." The voice becomes steadier, the caller gaining confidence. It has a familiar, resonant quality. "And now I *have* got a girlfriend, who's the best friend I've ever had, and her last relationship was a complete disaster zone, and now I'm going to go and break her heart as well."

Lily and Coral have dropped everything, literally onto the floor in some cases, and are staring at the radio as if it is a recently unpinned grenade. 'Derek' takes a gulp of hysterical air. "I hate myself! I've been so self-absorbed that I didn't consider that trying to please my mum could hurt a third party. I don't know if my girlfriend will ever be able to forgive me, but that's not really the point." Lily grabs her mobile phone.

"Lils, he's on the phone to the radio," Coral points out, her voice trembling; so Lily has to endure a few agonising minutes of sound advice before she can give the assurance she is longing to give.

Finally, the radio host says, "I hope this has been helpful. Goodbye, Derek," and moves onto the next caller. Lily holds down the number 2 on her phone, and presses it to her ear.

"Hi, Derek, it's Liljana. I was listening to the radio, and I forgive you absolutely and unconditionally, and I mean that one hundred percent. Now, go and be gay with Justin."

How obvious it now seems! How could Lily have missed what Tonia was talking about? *How did Tonia know?*

"Oh, Lily, I am so, so sorry. I don't know why I got involved with you, apart from that you're kind and funny and intelligent and, unlike me, were on the correct side of the mental health table."

Amos is still in tears, yet no less eloquent than usual. Gay, gay, gay. A maturely dressed, singing, St Pauli-supporting drama student! It was more obvious than Jacek being Polish!

"Not sure about that last point, Amos. Now I think about it, you couldn't be gayer if you tried, and the fact that I didn't notice says a lot about my mental condition."

"Chatting you up was a fairly good disguise, I guess, although you now know why I wasn't very comfortable in bed." He pauses for a second, then, in a small voice, adds, "Girls' bits are interesting, though." It seems, from the peals of laughter at Lily's end, that it wasn't too soon for a joke.

"So, are you still on for Saturday's more-than-solidarity exercise?"

"Definitely. And I'm going to ask you to take a big photo of me demonstrating against fascist bigots, so I can send it to my fascist bigot family. They need to wake the hell up."

Lily decides she will try and tone down his response when she sees him on Saturday, rather than on the phone. She doesn't want him to go to war with his parents, although she agrees that they need to be told. "Okay. See you outside the SU at eleven. Are we friends?"

"That's your decision. I don't expect you to forgive…"

"Best friends. Sleep better tonight than you have in ages, Derek," she says genuinely.

She hangs up, and falls into Coral's outstretched arms with an almighty, resigned sigh and a mutter of, "*Obviously* he was bloody well gay. What was I thinking?"

* * *

"I'm swearing off men until I've finished uni," announces Lily at the breakfast table the next day. "I know it's only two months, but I'd like to get this First because I can, even though I don't really have to anymore."

"And because you're more upset about breaking up with Amos than you're letting on," says Coral perceptively.

"Yeah, that."

On the way to work, Lily starts to feel worse. Heartbreak lodges in her stomach like a stodgy potato, making her dread the things she usually looks forward to. Although Lily's mum is nice, they had the usual awkwardness in their relationship when Lily was an adolescent; ever since year ten, when Lily had to tell Lucy that she wasn't going out with Luke Myerscough anymore, she has hated telling people about break-ups. It wounds her pride, and it is making her dread seeing Jacek. Of course, when she does see him, the potato and the adrenaline rush compete; a very strange and painful emotion results, which leaves Lily feeling light-headed.

"How's the naughty girl today?"

"Behaving until she graduates!"

"What does Amos say about that?"

"That he'd rather date our friend Justin."

"Pardon? What has happened? Tell me everything!" demands Jacek. Lily does. His reaction is amazing. He hugs her around the shoulders and says, "You don't deserve all this bad luck. Did you walk under a ladder?"

"I think walking under ladders is only damaging because ladders may fall on top of you, Jacek," says Lily, but she is smiling now. "Thank you, as always, for being perfect."

"I'm not perfect," Jacek mock-grumbles – his perfection, or lack of it, has been the subject of many a discussion between them. The trouble with Lily, he thinks to himself as he walks away, is that, in her company above all others, perfection is impossible. Look at him – he'd been a good, monogamous boy until she showed up, although in no way does he blame her for his indiscretion. Now she is single again – obviously, she thought his life was low on temptation and needed a bit more. How very inconsiderate of her.

*　　*　　*

"Okay, psychic Tonia, spill." Lily is on the sofa at her house, after work that night. She went round there as soon as she finished, because she needs to know.

"My mum is a fundamentalist, and my brother is gay," says Tonia simply. "I've known all my life… well, as soon as I was old enough to realise what gay was, I knew that Aaron was gay. He was never interested in anything stereotypically masculine. Didn't like team sports. Wasn't interested in competing. Would never join in all that 'We won, we won, and you lost,' singing on Sports Day – always wandered off and made daisy chains. Seriously, daisy chains, when he was thirteen." She throws back her head and laughs. "I was in year ten at the time, and when I saw him doing it, I wandered over and asked if he really wanted his head kicked in. You don't have younger siblings, so you don't know how frustrating it is when they're being dorky at school, and you know they're going to get a hard time, and you want to protect them, but you also know it's wrong just to tell them to be like everybody else…" She sighs.

"So when did he tell your mum, and what happened?" Lily asks.

"They haven't spoken since."

"That's horrible! What part of the Bible says don't talk to people who don't agree with you?"

"Well, quite," says Tonia flatly, "but people like my mum and her church have a way of twisting vaguely related verses to fit not having anything to do with people they don't like. Take Hebrews, for example: 'Resist the devil, and he will flee from you.' That's supposed to be about getting rid of your own sin, but they take it to mean avoiding the company of anyone they think is 'caught in a sin'. You'd think Jesus' command to love your enemies and pray for people who persecute you might trump a completely unrelated verse in Hebrews, but not according to my family…"

She pulls at a thread on one of Heidi's home-made cushions. "To be honest, Aaron isn't completely innocent in all this. He basically marched in one Sunday last year, an hour or so after Mum and Dad came from a big gift day at the church, tired but happy, and told them he was gay, and if they didn't like it he'd leave and never speak to them again. They quoted the Bible at him for about half an hour, hoping to change his mind – about being gay, not about not speaking to them. They didn't want to speak to him either, if he wouldn't 'repent' of being gay. Mum was down on her knees begging him not to 'exchange the truth of God for a lie'." Tears begin to slip down Tonia's face, and Lily hugs her close.

"Sorry, Lils. I've never told anyone about this before – not in so much detail. I gave Heidi the bare bones when it happened.

"That's okay," says Lily. "I hope Amos listens to me. He's planning to barrack his parents in much the same way you've just described. I can understand the compulsion to do that, but really, he should tell them calmly in the first instance, and wait to see if they'll be reasonable. He'll feel better about himself if he does."

"Exactly," sniffs Tonia. "Anyway, to cut a long story short, I'm the only one who's speaking to Aaron, and Mum grills me for information about his life every time I go home. She doesn't think she's being the slightest bit hypocritical, cutting someone off, but wanting to know about everything he does."

"Everyone's a hypocrite," observes Lily, although, as the girls fall into comfortable silence and focus on the television, she can't quite decide how and whether Jacek fits into this sweeping generalisation.

17

Graduation day!

Two and a half months have passed since the Amos debacle. Lily's man-avoidance did wonders – she got a First! Her mother and father were not expecting this. Lily has a history of getting Bs when she should get As, because she doesn't usually work very hard. She reflects that in the past there have been too many things taking her mind off work, but this year she has needed work to take her mind off things. Not necessarily unpleasant things, although some were undeniably so, but sometimes she has worked hard in order to get out of Jacek Land, and stop all her adrenaline supply from running out.

All the girls have passed well. Tonia is staying on in Southampton to do a Master's degree in Medieval and Renaissance Culture; Simon, whose degree is in Music, will also be on the inter-departmental course. Heidi has got a job as a research assistant for a Leeds-based publishing house. Coral and Lily are still looking for jobs. The best thing is that because Heidi's job doesn't start until mid-August, when the present incumbent will go on maternity leave, the girls are going to be able to go travelling together. They will leave on the first of July.

After being awarded her certificate, and having a hat placed precariously on her hair (which is in its second of two available styles; up) by the Vice Chancellor, Lily collects her mum and dad and goes to one of several marquees. There, Dan and Grandma Samson join them; they watched the ceremony over a video link. Heidi, Tonia and Coral are soon present, and there are many introductions and much photo-taking by people's mums.

"I love your skirt, Mrs. Banda," says Lily to Tonia's mum. It is a kind of sarong, tied at the waist, with a bold design of those African shields that look like surfboards.

"Thank you. It is called a *chitenje*, from Malawi. My husband is Malawian; I am Ghanaian, so I always seem to wear something from each country. My headdress is from Ghana, as you can probably guess. Tonia says you are unusually good at African geography." The scarf is red, yellow and green – the colours of the Ghanaian flag.

"I like to take an interest in world affairs," smiles Lily politely.

"Yes – it's really boring," jokes Tonia, and she and Lily manage to play-fight without getting champagne, or Tonia's parentally-sanctioned orange juice, on anyone's gown or *chitenje*.

"So, what are you going to do now you've graduated, Lily?" asks Coral's mum, Angela. Lily has met her many times before, due to staying at Coral's house for a few days during most holidays. Angela is large, and dresses in a feminine, slightly artistic way, like Coral. She looks and behaves a bit like Julie Walters as Molly Weasley.

"Not sure yet," Lily replies. "I applied for a few jobs, and never even had a reply – and I'm good at applications, so I can only blame the recession, and keep trying. Still, Hope's are keeping my job open for me while I travel, so I won't be short of money while I'm looking."

"Wouldn't it be cheaper to live at home?" Angela asks.

"A little, but as I'll be working full-time instead of part-time, it won't be a big difference, and I'm going to move in with Tonia, as Heidi is moving back to Leeds. The rent is cheaper than what Coral and I pay. Plus, I won't have to get on a hovercraft every time I have an interview, and I think, psychologically, employers might see moving off an island as a barrier to relocation."

The party breaks up then. Lily exchanges hugs with her friends, they all remind each other to meet at 7pm at Victoria Station on the first of July, and everybody wanders off with their families. Lily's idea of a family meal isn't fancy, so they head towards Piccolo Mondo, a rustic, affordable and very friendly restaurant in the town centre. However, as the McGoldrick-Samson family approach the exit opening of the marquee, a tall, blond young man approaches them. In his arms is a bunch of orange lilies, with a splendid pink one at the centre. He smiles as the family approaches.

"Sorry I'm late, Lily. I wanted to congratulate you on your graduation. Hope you don't mind."

Lily is always pleased to see Jacek, and is particularly thrilled right now. "Jacek, you are amazing, and these flowers are beautiful. Mum, Dad, this is Jacek Bogdanowski – the cause of, and solution to, all of life's problems," she says, paraphrasing Homer Simpson.

"Hello, Jacek," says Saint Lucy – the solution to all problems caused by Jacek – very warmly. "We've heard so much about how supportive you have been of Lily, and I'm glad to be able to say thank you in person."

"Lily has been exaggerating again, I am sure of it," says Jacek firmly, taking Saint Michael outstretched hand equally firmly.

This handshake is the main topic of conversation en route to the restaurant, after Jacek is introduced to Dan and Grandma, and declines an offer to join the family for dinner.

"He's got a Vulcan death grip, that Pole," jokes Michael. "I do hope he wasn't trying to show me who's boss."

"Don't be silly, Dad, he's like that with everybody," giggles Lily, who has butterflies in her stomach and bouncing flowers in her arms. "Doesn't know his own strength."

"Does he know his own strength when he pins you to the bed and…"

"Daniel Patrick McGoldrick!"

"Sorry, Mum."

* * *

"So, how do you know I like pink and orange flowers? Lily asks Jacek at work the next day.

She's limping a little, having sprained her ankle while moving into Tonia's flat earlier that day. Sally has dispatched Lily to the office so that Lynn, who has just been trained as a First Aider, can look at her ankle. Jacek is in there because he has some stock control forms to fill in.

"You always wear pink, orange and red," observes Jacek. "The colours of the top of the rainbow."

"Pink is at the bottom, isn't it?"

"Only if there is blue in it."

"Which would technically be purple," observes Lily. "I guess you're right."

"Fuchsia," says Lynn, administering an elastic bandage.

"I thought that was pronounced…"

"Jacek!"

"Sorry, Lynn."

"Anyway," says Lily, "I always wear blue when you see me." She indicates her uniform.

"Try walking on that," says Lynn, admiring her handiwork.

Lily gets up and walks in the direction of Jacek, staggering less than before. At that moment, Sue calls Lynn over to try to explain why her computer's screen has suddenly turned a fetching shade of fuchsia, and so Lynn doesn't see the fruit of her labours.

"Your pyjamas are pink," whispers Jacek to Lily, out of earshot of all the others. "Your favourite T-shirt, with the seahorse on, is orange. Your stupid Arsenal shirts are red, as is your sexy Christmas dress. Will I be seeing it again?"

"What? What about me in my woolly nightie?" demands Lynn, rejoining the conversation. Everybody bursts out laughing, including Sue, whose computer screen is now the shade people expect to see when something is wrong: blue.

18

The first of July seems to take ages to arrive, and then to have taken no time at all once it does – this is life.

"Hieee!" squeal Lily and Tonia, as they arrive at Victoria Coach Station to find Heidi and Coral already waiting. Coral is picking guiltily at a Danish and staring disconsolately at her skinny latte, and Heidi is eating Burger King with no shame whatsoever. Coral forgets her troubles as soon as she sees her friends, and it's hugs all round.

"What have you been doing these last few weeks?" asks Tonia, not looking at anyone in particular.

Heidi says, "Eating chips and playing rugby. You don't do chips properly down south. They're too thin and crispy. You've conflated chips with those poncy Italian-style pizzas that don't make you put on enough weight."

"You're not going to lose any weight in Italy, Heidi," says Coral. "Trust me. I went to Milan with Kayli" – her friend from secondary school in London – "last summer, and we bought an ice-cream sundae that cost fifteen Euros. It was huge, and came in an edible peanut brittle basket. We couldn't finish it." Coral has been on a bathing-suit diet, hence currently being unable to stop thinking about food.

"I've been working, and watching Euro 2012, says Lily. Tonia sighs.

"What?" demands Lily, knowing full well what.

"You haven't been watching Euro 2012, just Italy. And Balotelli."

"Is that a crime?" Coral, who has also been watching Mario Balotelli, interjects.

"No! Exactly!" says Lily triumphantly. "*Anyway*, so the Euros have been nice and shirtless, and work hasn't been too bad. Jacek remembers what colour my pyjamas are."

"Pardon?" says Coral.

"I asked him how he knows I like pink and orange flowers..."

"And he based his choice on your pyjamas? Not very sexy, is it? What about your bra?" interrupts Heidi.

"Shh! I thought it was romantic. Anyway, my bra was black. How many flowers are black?"

"Black roses," observes Tonia. "Simon gave me those for our six-month anniversary. Jacek's such a Goth, I thought those would be the obvious choice."

"You can't give roses to your ex-girlfriend when you've got another one," argues Lily.

"I've written a cookbook!" interjects Coral, anxious to get the conversation back on track.

"Really? What kind?"

"Well, in April, I suddenly decided that a Euro 2012 cookbook would be a good idea – recipes from every country, but it was too late to start. So, instead, I've been working on a Champions League cookbook, prospective release date August the 24th – the date of the group stage draw. My sister did the photography. I've licensed the work under a Creative Commons Licence, and phoned UEFA in Switzerland to ask if they would endorse it. I had to speak French, which was embarrassing... Anyway, I'm waiting for their call."

"What if they refuse to endorse it, and also say you can't do it?" worries Tonia, the most levelheaded of the girls, aloud.

"Then I'll change the name. I'm thinking of Matchday Magic. It's full of practical ideas for food that you can make between getting home from work at 6.30 and your friends coming over for the match at 7.15, and it's all eatable in front of the telly. Plus, there's some recipes for food that you can take to the game with you, and even some meals that you can *make at half time*. I've tested them."

"How come I never noticed you recipe testing in our flat?" demands Lily.

"You were so into your revision, and you thought I was too. Sorry for not telling you, but you know I'm superstitious about big projects. Telling people about them seems to be directly linked to not finishing them."

"No problem. I'm very excited for you!"

"I've been working too, and saving for the ridiculous university reading list next year." Tonia works at New Look in Southampton city centre. "They want us to read every medieval book that survives, plus a ton of linguistic history, and all this theory about the social causes of language development. I haven't done any sociology since A level, so it's going to be fun."

"I bet you were good at it, though," says Coral.

"Well, yes, okay. My sister hates me for not choosing sociology for my degree. She says I had to go and choose the one thing she was good at, literature, and get even better at it than her. I'm sure that she's going to apply for a four year PhD soon, so that I can never be more qualified than her."

"Would pass..." (crackle) "France please check in at the Euro..." (crackle) "immediately."

"That's our cue to exit... I think," says Lily, who has become an expert in terrible PA message interpretation thanks to her job at Hope's.

All four girls head to the Eurolines check-in desk, passports in hands, tickets in passports, and butterflies in stomachs. The adventure has begun.

Paris

"Did anyone else bring Euro change?"

"No, Lily. I know you told us to, but we forgot."

"This always happens," mutters Lily. "Why can't you put notes in these machines, like you can in England?"

The girls eventually buy breakfast pastries from a relatively expensive station kiosk, and then use the change to buy their day passes for the Metro. Coral's doesn't make the ticket gate open.

"*Le machine n'aime pas mon billet*!" she splutters to the barrier operator, who checks its validity, then opens the gate manually to let her through.

"I keep having to speak French all the time at the moment! Do you think it's a sign?" Coral asks her friends.

"Being French would suit you," observes Heidi. "You like arty-farty cooking, and you dress nicely. You'd also never have to think about low-fat products again. I'm not sure they exist here."

"In Paris, they might," says Tonia. "All the models… I think Coral might prefer the south of France. The laid-back lifestyle, the two-hour lunches with an inch of wine in your glass at all times…"

"And a Robert Pires clone for a husband?" suggests Coral cheekily. "Sold! When can I move?"

Everyone always says Paris is expensive, but it's really only on a par with London, and some things – taxis, the Metro, wine – are considerably cheaper.

"All the same, we *are* on a travel budget," says Tonia anxiously. "We need to watch our spending."

"Yeah, but not on the first day, says Heidi. "You're supposed to waste money then, and ask questions later."

The girls are clothes shopping, but not in a boutiquey tourist-in-Paris way – more in a young French student way. There are chains that don't exist at home, with high street fashions that are different from those in the UK, at very reasonable prices. Lily buys a long, black and white, vertical-striped thing that is sleeveless and made of wool, and therefore useless.

"But it's seven Euros fifty worth of useless, and I've never seen anything like it at home," she says firmly. "Also, I'll never be able to go to that shop again, because it's for young women – I had to take the top size."

She suffers from one of her increasingly rare pangs of sadness; if she hadn't lost the baby, such clothes would have been beyond her reach forever. Illogically, she now feels guilty about the purchase.

"I still maintain that it's a top," says Tonia.

"Dress!"

"Top!"

"If it covers my bum, it's a dress," says Lily defiantly.

"It only covers your bum because you're not normal. It's a top," says Heidi.

"She *is* normal. She's five foot six and a size ten. That's normal, if you're going into a young women's fashion shop. You're the one that's not normal. It would be a top on you, or a vest on me," says Coral.

Neither Heidi – due to her height – nor Coral managed to find anything to fit in that shop. Lily, being incredibly nice, tried on and paid for the dress very quickly to spare Coral's feelings.

That evening, after a very reasonably priced – and beautifully cooked – meal in a small family-run restaurant, the girls end up in the Auld Alliance, as hundreds of thousands of young British backpackers have before them. It is a Scottish pub. The staff are friendly, and keen to talk to the girls about their future destinations.

"Hamburg? Great nightlife. Livorno? Why would you want to… Oh, I get it. Hamburg, Livorno… Glasgow next stop, is it?" The barman, Adrian, grins cheekily at Lily. "Rome? *You'll* hate it, *you'll* hate it, you two'll be OK."

(I won't reveal just now which girls he was pointing at when he spoke, but he was only half right.)

Milan

"Heidi, *why* did you have to buy that water-carrier statue in Hamburg? It weighs a ton."

"I like it, Tonia, and I didn't ask you to put it in your suitcase…"

"Did I have a choice?"

Heidi's suitcase is already packed out with souvenirs for her parents, grandparents and four siblings. She's considering a trip to the post office to dispatch some of it home, although she doesn't really want to, as it will spoil the surprise.

"Right," says Lily decisively, as they arrive at their small hotel. "Coral, you've been here before. What didn't you get around to doing?"

But Coral isn't listening, because the proprietor of the hotel has just arrived, and rooms tend to fall silent when he enters them. Or at least they would if he didn't live in Milan, where everyone is gorgeous. He has light brown hair, and the most incredible sea-green eyes. He is about thirty years old. In spite of his beauty, he seems approachable; there is something encouraging about his demeanour.

"*Buongiorno. Ho prenotato*," manages Lily.[1] It's Coral's line, but she's dumbstruck.

"What is your name?" he asks, with only a very slight accent.

"We're booked in under Lily McGoldrick."

"Okay, passports, please." Lily wonders if foreign nationals have to surrender their passports when they arrive in the UK. The girls have had to do it in every country thus far.

"Here are your room keys. Two twin rooms. One on the ground floor" – he indicated the room right behind his desk – "one on the first floor. This way, please."

He turns, and begins to unlock the ground floor room, failing to see the almighty struggle that ensues, which Coral wins by implanting her elbow in Heidi's ribs. Coral may abhor exercise of every kind, but she is mysteriously strong.

"Okay, which of you… ah." Lily and Coral already have a foot each in the door. The Italian therefore turns to Tonia and Heidi. "This way, please, ladies."

And so the losing pair are escorted upstairs by a gorgeous Italian for their trouble – not a bad consolation prize.

It turns out that Coral, for reasons known only to herself, did not complete a tour of the San Siro last time she was here.

"I was with Kayli. She wouldn't have approved." Kayli's sport avoidance, unlike Coral's, extends to watching.

"Well, let's go, then," says Lily decisively. "Oh, wait…" She re-enters the hotel room, and emerges wearing her Arsenal shirt. "I'm ready now."

The stadium is amazing. The museum contains several life-size waxworks of former players, including a goalkeeper

---

[1] Good day. I have a reservation.

called Cudicini, who, it transpires, is Carlo Cudicini's father. Best of all, there is one of Paolo Maldini. Photography is forbidden, which Coral ignores.

"I can't not have one of me and Paolo, can I?... I wonder what Hotel Bloke's name is? I'll have to ask him before I leave."

The dressing rooms are puzzling. AC Milan's home dressing room is the height of luxury. Players have padded seats with their own numbers on. There is a scramble to sit on Alessandro Nesta's first; Heidi wins, making up for her loss to Coral over the room. On the other hand, Internazionale's players have to make do with a solid hard plastic ring to sit together on.

"What if you were Ronaldo, or Patrick Vieira, and had played for both clubs? What would you think?" asks Coral excitedly.

"I don't think Vieira was senior enough at Milan to have had his own seat number," says Lily knowledgeably. "I see your point, though. Perhaps it's a disincentive to commit such a terrible betrayal? It'd only work as a disincentive for the Milan players, though. Is it a conspiracy by Berlusconi?"

"The seats in the Tottenham dressing room should be on *fire*, then" says Tonia decisively.

Near the stadium is a very large statue of a horse. Leonardo da Vinci apparently designed it but never built it, so twentieth century architects decided to build it as a tribute.

"It would be fun to climb," says Heidi deviously.

"No," says Tonia.

"Why not? You jump into lakes!"

"I wouldn't jump into water in Italy. I hear tourists get arrested for jumping in the Trevi fountain. Anyway, I'm Malawian. Lakes are in my blood."

"And promiscuity is in Lily's, and eating in Coral's," says Heidi decisively.

"I'm not promiscuous!" says Lily indignantly.

"How many boyfriends have you had?"

"Six, but I slept with one, three times! I don't call three shags with one man in six years of having boyfriends promiscuous, do you?"

"Yeah, but how many men have seen you naked?" asks Heidi slyly.

Mumble.

"Louder, please, Lily."

"Six."

"See? You expose yourself to everyone. How many men have seen you naked, Tonia?"

"Not counting my dad or brother? Only one. Simon."

"Coral?"

"Two, but that's because of lack of opportunity. I'm not *against* being seen naked."

"Four for me, so Lily, you really are the naughtiest of them all!" sings Heidi triumphantly.

"Which is *fine*," say Coral and Tonia in unison, and then they look at each other and laugh.

"I never said it wasn't. Just telling the truth."

* * *

"Why do I do it, do you think?" Lily asks Tonia later. "I mean, I'm a Christian. I really am. I know God is in my life, and I know I shouldn't do these things. So why do I do it?"

"Well… I know God is in my life, too, and I'm not *having sex* with Simon, but I'm still doing stuff with him that God and my mother would say is wrong. I think we get brought up with this idea that *intercourse* is wrong, so we think, 'Okay, I just won't have intercourse'. By the time you go to a Christian youth meeting and find out that everything else is wrong as well, it's too late. You've either already done it, or want it too much not to do it, because you've thought about what it might be like."

"So," says Lily, "are we saying that sex ed, plus what we get told in church before we're sixteen is focused too much on shagging, and ignores the fact that most of what unmarried couples do isn't shagging, but contains all the same emotional responsibilities – just not the physical ones?"

"Yes," Tonia agrees. "There's so much focus on preventing pregnancy and STIs. In church, you get told that having sex makes two become one in the sight of God, and is a sin against the body, but they never address 'how far can we go?' until you've already made an uninformed choice."

"Parents don't help, either," muses Lily. "If you can't be good, be careful; if you can't be careful, be good, they say. They never explain how being careful can be bad. I don't think my parents even think it's bad, although I know they're true Christians too."

"And if you do ask how far you can go, some smug, 'mature' Christian will always say that it's the wrong question, and that if you have the Holy Spirit, you'll know the answer. But, even though I gave my life to Jesus when I was ten, I never felt like *doing stuff* was bad, until somebody said so at Soul Survivor. Sometimes, I think it's the church that makes me feel bad about what I do with Simon, not God."

The two girls fall silent, watching the sun set in central Milan as the remains of their fifteen Euro ice creams melt into expensive milkshakes.

Rome

The girls never did find out the name of the hotel guy, thanks to too many late nights and early mornings. They did find out that he still lives with his mum.

"Surely a sign of the ridiculousness of Milan," observes Lily. "A man like that would get snapped up in three seconds' flat in the UK. We should have encouraged him to move to London."

"Or shoved him into Heidi's suddenly empty suitcase," giggles Tonia. Heidi gave up on her 'surprise' presents after deciding she was unable to live without an Italian rugby shirt and half a Milanese boutique.

In Milan, Lily had found that her French jumper-dress was the only acceptable wardrobe item she had. The women in Milan dressed in monochromatic, conservative-but-stylish clothes; even Coral had felt deeply unfashionable there, due to her love of glorious colours.

"At least all the *normal* girls there were my size," says Coral now, referring to those few that didn't look like professional models. "I can see why, too. All they do is eat!"

"All *we* did was eat," corrects Tonia, whose Parisian little-girl shop purchases no longer fit.

"No, she's right!" insists Lily. "The Italian culture involves eating a three- or four-course meal every night at around eight or nine in the evening. It's a silly way to eat, but they love it – and some parts of Italy have the longest life expectancy in the world."

"It's a low saturated fat diet," observes Heidi.

Beep! A car has made a ridiculous U-turn near the café where the girls are sitting. Furious motorists are gesticulating at the driver, who sticks his head out of the window of his car and yells back at them.

"I saw a funny YouTube video about this once," says Lily. "Some self-deprecating Italians had made it, comparing their driving, politics and other things unfavourably to the rest of Europe."

Beep!

The girls expect to see another near-death experience on the road, but not this time. Instead, a man sticks his head out of the window and blows a kiss at Heidi.

"Interesting," she says, after he has driven away again. "Lower standards here than in Milan, obviously."

"*Different* standards," says Coral. "There, they like their typical national appearance. Here, they are looking for something different."

*   *   *

"*Ciao, bella!*"

"Twenty-one." Heidi has taken to counting her admirers.

"None of them have been very hot so far, though," muses Coral.

"That's normal. What percentage of men are hot in any city that's not Milan? They all seem to be very confident here, though," says Lily.

"I wonder how they behave with Italian women?" Tonia wonders aloud.

"Probably, they tread more carefully," Heidi supposes. "An Italian woman might be a future wife. Blondes are clearly tourists. It's all just a bit of harmless fun."

* * *

"Are we going to do the stadium tour?" asks Lily, expecting a chorus of yeses.

"Do we have to?"

Tonia's three friends turn to her in surprise. "Are you sick of looking at football grounds?" ventures Coral.

"No. I just don't fancy meeting… those people Lily doesn't like."

"Irriducibili? I wouldn't worry about them too much. It's the close season. Anyway, if they're all like Paolo di Canio, they'll only be fascist bastards, rather than fascist and racist ones. I know that's not great news for the human race, but it's better than nothing."

"But, if you're really worried, we'll all stay away in sympathy," says Heidi, and everyone nods in agreement.

In the end, the girls do visit the Stadio Olimpico, and no right-wing Ultras make themselves known visibly or audibly. The tour guide is a Roma supporter who makes the hot guy from the hotel in Milan look like Wayne Rooney. About twenty tourists are in their group, and the majority are female – mostly with husbands or boyfriends, save a pair of American students, who get on very well with their British counterparts. One of them is called Elizabeth Wu, which makes Tonia feel better – at least she won't have to face any rogue Irriducibili alone. There is much giggling over Benito, the tour guide.

"Do you think he's really Benito Carbone?" asks Lily, who has the longest memory, not to mention an older brother who likes his football.

"He's better looking, and twenty years younger, than Benito Carbone," Tonia points out.

"Who's Benito Carbone?" asks Elizabeth's friend Mavis.

"Used to play for Bradford City when I was about ten. Had long hair. My brother's girlfriend at the time supports Bradford to this day, because of him. I saw her wearing her Bradford shirt down the high street in Ryde, when I was home for Easter."

"Do you live near Bradford?" asks Mavis pleasantly, clearly not following the conversation.

"*Possimo avere la tua numero di telefona*?" says Benito.

"It means he wants your number, Heidi," hisses Coral, and everyone else adopts an expression somewhere between astonishment and glee, comprising open mouths and smiling eyes.

After the tour, all six students end up in a café. "Let's play a game," says Elizabeth. She attempts to call a waiter.

"*Scusi!*" He ignores her. She tries another. "*Scusi!*" He is simultaneously summoned by another table, and chooses that one, but returns to their table straight after.

"*Il menu, per favore?*" asks Elizabeth.

"*Si,*" the waiter replies, nodding to them all as he disappears. When he returns with three menus for the six of them to share, Elizabeth says, "Now it's Mavis' turn, but first, decide what you want to eat."

All six girls choose, then Mavis summons a waiter. "*Scusi!*" He immediately turns and beams at her, notepad in hand.

"They *love* non-Italian looking girls," explains Mavis when he is gone, "but Chinese is going too far. Elizabeth's more confident than me, and when we first came, she was asking for everything, and the slow service frustrated us. One day, she got a phone call just as we wanted to order, and I called a waiter. Snap – he was here in a trice."

"Was that always in this place?"

"In Rome, yes," says Mavis, who is proving to be a little on the slow side.

"No," says Lily, "I meant in this bar. Do you mean to say that Italian waiters favour you over Elizabeth everywhere you go in Rome?"

"Uh-huh."

"Didn't you notice?" asks Tonia, playing with a napkin.

"Pardon?" says Lily.

"What happens when *we* ask for things."

"Well, Coral usually asks, doesn't she? Anyway, we get served pretty quickly, thanks to our lucky mascot." Lily pats Heidi on the head.

"I had a similar experience to Elizabeth's," says Tonia, quietly. "Yesterday, in that trattoria, everyone needed the loo except me – do you remember? You asked me to order, and when you returned, you asked why I hadn't. Well, I tried to, four times. One waiter even went to the same table twice in five minutes, leaving me alone."

"Why didn't you say?" demands Lily. "We'd have left."

"I don't like to draw attention to those sorts of problems," says Tonia. "Look around you – very few black people. If someone who looks like me doesn't serve you on a checkout every day, or – better still – sit next to you at work, we remain a mystery, and people are generally afraid of mysteries."

"That's the second amazingly deep thing you've said in a week, Tonia," smiles Lily, mildly awestruck. Tonia usually thinks 'deep' is an abbreviated word for 'boring'.

"Yes, and I don't like it. When can we get out of Italy? It's making me go funny."

"We have to go to Livorno first," Lily decrees. "Sorry, but that's one of my must-dos." She turns to the Americans. "Would you like to come to Livorno with us?"

"Ugh, no! Livorno's full of Communists," says Elizabeth, askance.

"Yes, hence they'll accept you for who you are, unlike the conservatives and fascists here in Rome," says Lily. "Anyway, I'm a socialist. Do you hate me now?"

"No, because you're British."

"And Livorno socialists are Italians. Does that make them bad?"

"What Elizabeth means," says Mavis earnestly, "is that in Britain, socialism is part of the culture. Even if a British person is sexist and racist, they probably still believe that things like healthcare, education and clean water are basic rights. Here in Italy, socialism is hardcore, and so is fascism. People believe in totally changing world systems, and getting rid of democracy. In the US, being conservative doesn't mean being racist. It means believing in the free market, and that individuals should take responsibility for their own lives."

Interesting – Mavis obviously isn't stupid, thinks Lily. *She just seems to need a little longer than everybody else to absorb information, but when she has done so, it comes out very eloquently.*

"I think you're wrong about 'hardcore socialists' wanting to get rid of democracy," says Lily. "I think we aspire to a higher form of democracy. Representation has failed. Parties listen to their millionaire donors, rather than ordinary voters, and tear up their manifestoes the day after each election. You then get four years of policies you didn't vote for, on the premise that you voted for the individual, or the party, to have power."

"This is boring," says Tonia. "Can we go and do something fun now?"

* * *

"Are you packed?" Lily asks Tonia, as she walks into the hostel canteen for breakfast.

"Yes, but Heidi isn't." They exchange knowing looks. The previous night, the four British girls and their new American friends partied until dawn. Heidi had invited Benito along, wandered off with him, and strolled into the hostel just in time for an early breakfast, which she eschewed in favour of a shower and a couple of hours' sleep.

"Good job she's only got a Roma shirt to add to her inventory," smirks Lily. It was a present from Benito, gratefully received, as the girls are indulging fully in hating Lazio.

Tonia, Lily and Coral have just poured milk over their cornflakes and grapefruit when Heidi appears.

"Afternoon, Heidi," says Coral.

"Five," says Heidi.

"Naughty Heidi," giggles Lily.

"It's not six, is it, Lily?"

"But it will be, unless you marry Benito – and I'm determined not to get past seven!"

Southampton

The odyssey is over. Lily's new second favourite country is now Croatia, behind Poland. Tonia's second favourite city is now Paris, behind London. Lily is ironing her Hope's uniform; Tonia is reading a tome called, "Studies in Medieval Language and Culture". There's an essay due in the second week or term, before much teaching has been done – which seems grossly unfair, especially given how much a taught Masters costs.

"Are you glad to be back, Tonia?"

"No. I want to go back to Paris, don't you?"

Tonia loves the global cities; it is now her ambition to visit Tokyo and New York. Lily knows that this is partly because a black woman can visit these cities and feel normal, and feels a mixture of sympathy, anger and irrational guilt. She doesn't feel comfortable knowing that her skin is a second passport, something that will enable her to fit in anywhere in Europe. Such respect should be earned, thinks Lily, or given on rational grounds.

"Well," she says, in answer to her flatmate's question, "I miss it, but I'm always a bit glad to be home. I wish I was *home* home, though, not going back to work. I might never default to my parents' house again, you realise."

"Any news on jobs in the mail?"

"My first rejection letter, in four months of applications."

"Did you go to see the…"

"Careers Office? Yes. They said my CV is great, that I should tweak it to suit the individual job, and that my covering letter style is fine. They said my 'addiction to solidarity' would count as a plus point to some employers, and a minus to others – which is fine, as I'd rather not work for Tories."

Amos' description of Lily's political activism has entered her vernacular, and that of all her friends.

"You might not have a choice in the end, thanks to the Tories and their idea of 'getting out of' a recession."

"Have you been eating political bread? You're scaring me!"

"I keep thinking about what Mavis said," says Tonia, "and I think she was wrong. Being conservative… I think it *is* racist, because it means you support the status quo, and black people are currently relatively poor in every white majority country. I read once that most American evangelical Christians are Republicans, unless they're black. That means something. It's all very well to believe in taking responsibility for yourself if you've never been discriminated against for a stupid reason. It's easy to work hard, and get what you want, if you have the same background and interests as your line manager. That's how white supremacy survives, even when people aren't racist on purpose."

"I'm getting a new bread bin," declares Lily, "or asking Hope's to change their recipe… Actually, I'm not. I like political bread-fed Tonia! Keep it up!"

19

"Would you consider applying for my job?"

"No, because you're not allowed to leave!" Jacek and Lily have run into each other on the way to work, in the newsagent's – her purchases, chocolate and a magazine, his, *The Mirror*.

"I'm not leaving. I'm applying for Sally's job. Did she tell you she's handed in her notice?"

"I haven't seen her."

"She may have written to you on Facebook. Derek Hill has employed her as an office manager." Derek is an engineer-turned Productivity Manager at a local tool-manufacturing firm. "It's a much better job than manager at Hope's. She is lucky."

"I think she realised how much the place had changed her," muses Lily. "Have you noticed that she keeps trying to be nice to people? She wants to get back to what she used to enjoy. Good on Derek for helping her out."

"Anyway, if I am successful, I will tell David that you are the best choice for grocery supervisor."

"I don't wanna be a grocery supervisor!" wails Lily. "But thank you for the thought. I think Lynn deserves a promotion. She's worked hard for two years, and she isn't being paid any extra for doing First Aid."

"Hmm, interesting. I will consider her, especially as she is saving for a wedding."

"What?"

Lily is walking into Hope's, thinking about how Tonia's theory of wanting to reward your own race only works if the different-raced supervisor isn't the nicest man in the world, when her eyes are drawn to a newcomer.

He wears the distinct uniform of Hope's security. He is Lily's age, maybe younger, with white-blond hair that is short, but not shaved. He has astonishing blue eyes. He is Lily's height, and probably her weight, too. He looks lively and restless. As soon as he sees her, he breaks into a mischievous smile. Lily likes him immediately.

"Hi," he says. "Are you new?"

"I think you're newer. I've been away for six weeks."

"Oh, I see. I started a month ago. Ryan James." He has a rough local accent, though London-esque, with just a hint of the strong 'r' pronunciation of the Southampton accent.

"I'm Lily McGoldrick. Hopefully, I won't be here to annoy you for very long. I just graduated."

"Ah, there's no jobs, are there?"

"Lily!" Lynn is walking towards her, beaming. "Great news! Frank and I are getting married!"

"Really? Frank from Security?" Lily hugs Lynn tightly. "That's amazing! I had no idea!"

"We kept it quiet. We didn't want gossip. He was so nice to me at that Christmas meal… His first wife died of malaria back in Kenya, so his story's less sordid than mine, but he doesn't judge people. We're very happy."

"So am I! When's the wedding?"

"Next August, at the Riverside Family Church. You'll be invited, of course."

Lily and Lynn go to clock in. Jacek has been talking to Jim about an incident the previous night. A drunk man had come in and smashed eighteen bottles of brandy because he thought the price was too high. In doing so, he ensured that he had to pay for them and wouldn't get to drink them, instead of buying something cheaper instead, as a sober person would have done. Jacek and Jim have been reconciled somewhat because Jacek is mellowing in his attitude to people's appearances.

A few minutes later, Ryan and Jacek end up walking side by side en route to the men's room.

"… And my little granddaughter's going to be just old enough to be a bridesmaid by then. And we're going to have a choice of English or African food at the reception."

"I'll take African, definitely! Do you have any idea what they eat in Kenya?"

"Nah. Frank prefers chips…"

Lily and Lynn drift out of earshot of Ryan and Jacek. As soon as they do, Ryan quietly says, “I don’t agree with it.”

“With marriage? I used to be unsure, but now I think it’s good,” says Jacek.

He’s been thinking about marriage, and what should and should not be eschewed until marriage, a lot. Part of him feels that he shouldn’t have taken Lily’s honour, and part of him likes to remember the occasion in full Technicolor.

“No, I mean race-mixing. Good job she’s probably too old to have kids, I say.”

“I don’t agree,” says Jacek simply, turning to go back downstairs. Better to get told off for using the customer toilets than to have to share a urinal with a moron.

20

"Hey, Lily!"

Ryan is waving to her in the canteen. Lily is alone for lunch; Jacek is having his interview for Sally's job, and Lynn only works a half-day on Saturdays. Lily has prayed hard for Jacek all morning, but doesn't think he needs help, really.

"Hey, how was your morning?" she replies.

"Bit boring, but I like working with Jim. He's sound! That other one – Frank – he's *so* boring..."

"I like Frank, but he is quiet. Very kind though, and funny when the mood takes him. Still waters run deep, as they say," replies Lily.

"What you got there?" He indicates her dinner.

"Chicken in white wine sauce."

"What are all the vegetables in aid of?" Ryan wrinkles his nose at the sight of her side dish.

"I didn't think it'd go with chips."

"Then get steak." He starts to saw at the lump of meat on his plate with difficulty.

"I'm not a fan of plain meat. I like it in a sauce. Anyway – you choose your accompaniment first, then the main course to go with it, rather than the other way round? Very odd..."

"I just have to have chips. Want one?"

Lily can't say no. "Thanks. Want some vegetables?" she responds, just to see the look on his face.

"No, thanks. I think I'll live on chips, at least until I get old and fat."

"Not a bad philosophy. Use your metabolism while you still have it. How old are you?"

"Nineteen. You must be twenty one."

Lily nods. "Twenty two on Firework Night."

"Wow," says Ryan, cheeky blue eyes full of mischief, "and a Scorpio to boot. You must be a fiery one."

"I'd say passionate."

"Even better!" He rubs his hands together with glee, then grabs a napkin to wipe off the chip fat that he's spread everywhere.

*   *   *

"There's a hot guy at work," Lily calls to Tonia when she gets home.

"Yes, we know. You've told us about a thousand times."

"Not that one. A new one… Oh, hi, Simon." The pair are heating up microwave meals.

"I must say, living with Coral was like paying for a chef," Lily teases. "I miss not having to come home from work, and then cook dinner."

"You can have one of these." Tonia picks one box at a time out of an Iceland bag, and waves each one at Lily before setting it down on the counter. "Chicken and chips, spaghetti Bolognese, chips and curry sauce…"

"I thought you used to cook, Tonia?"

"I did. Heidi showed me the light."

"Okay," says Lily with a resigned sigh, but she's smiling. "Well, may I deprive you of a chips and curry sauce? I'll fashion something to go with it." Lily busies herself with the contents of the freezer as Tonia asks questions.

"So, who's the hot new guy?"

"Ryan. He's nineteen. I hardly know him yet, but he seems pretty bouncy."

"Yeah, I think you need bouncy. What does he look like?"

"Five foot seven, blond and blue eyed, wiry. He plays as a winger for a non-League team, despite his strict diet of meat and chips."

"Sounds like Heidi's perfect man," Tonia remarks.

"Does she want a relationship over two hundred and fifty miles? I doubt it," shrugs Lily, punching buttons on the microwave.

"She's emailing Benito…"

"*Is* she now? I would have thought she'd have put that one to bed in Rome."

"No, she *took him* to bed in Rome," giggles Tonia. "She realised the other day that no one we saw on the holiday – not even that seven-foot guy in the six-foot lift in Zagreb – came close, so she's considering giving it a go."

"Wow, that'll be a departure for her – literally. He'll have trouble keeping her to himself in Rome, though. I think they need to move to a country where both of them look unremarkable," says Lily ruefully.

"There isn't one. They'd probably blend into Paris or Milan during fashion week, though."

"Not with her rugby shirt on, I take it?"

*   *   *

"What's that you're wearing, Lily?"

"A Livorno shirt."

"Not heard of that one," says Ryan, putting down his pint and pulling up a chair so that Lily can sit down.

They've met in the Mitre by coincidence. Ryan's mates have left, and he's waiting for his dad to pick him up and take him home for Sunday tea. Lily is meeting Jacek, Gabriela, Tonia and Simon in here for football.

"They're a socialist team. Well, their fans are socialist. The Italian Communist Party was formed in Livorno – it's an industrial port. Sorry, am I boring you?"

Ryan looks somewhat displeased. Unbeknown to Lily, his nineteen-year-old brain is saying to itself, 'Her politics might be revolting, but her body is not. Play along – you might get lucky.'

"Sorry," he says aloud, "I'm just not really into politics, so I couldn't follow. You support an English team too, though, right?"

"Yes – Arsenal."

"Ugh. What's wrong with Southampton?"

"Nothing, but I'm not from Southampton, and I've supported Arsenal since I was eight," explains Lily.

"Fair enough. Where are you from?"

"Ryde. I've been to see Ryde Sports play a few times."

"Actually, I've played against them three times. Well, coming from Ryde, your natural choice would be Portsmouth, so for avoiding that, I salute you." At this point, Mr James arrives, as do Tonia and Simon.

"Well, nice talking to you, Lily. I'll be off. See you at work."

Lily greets Tonia and Simon and waves goodbye to Ryan, who she sees getting into his dad's car through the window. She laughs. She's done that before – a skinny person's trick that always terrifies the driver. She is too far away to hear Ryan's father's racist description of Lily's friendship with Tonia, and his rant about how Ryan had better tread carefully with one who keeps such company.

* * *

"You want to date a socialist whose flatmate is black?" Ryan's friend Marcus is incredulous.

"You should see her. Almost as tall as me, this amazing soft brown hair, and big green eyes."

"She'll still be shot when our day comes," says Ian cheerfully, opening a bag of peanuts along the seam, so that his fellow right-wingers can share.

"I'm not going to turn into a socialist by shagging her. Don't you watch Top Gear? Socialist women are better in bed than Tory women."

"Yeah, but who do you think she might have already slept with? You might catch something," warns Ian.

"I think she might be" – Ryan affects a posh accent – "awfully well-behaved."

"If she's a virgin, she won't be any good in bed, and if she isn't, she's probably got AIDS," says Ian. "Don't go there."

"Blokes can't get AIDS from women," argues Marcus.

"They can, but it's harder… Why are we talking about this? I really don't think Lily's got AIDS!" says Ryan in exasperation.

"Okay, Ryan." Tom, the fourth and final regular attendee of Southampton National Front meetings, piles in after listening to the ribald debate. "Maybe you can shag her, and afterwards, maybe we can have fun with her."

"What did you have in mind?" asks Ryan, anxious to provide a justifiable context to his fascination with getting Lily into bed.

"Give me a minute. I'll think of something," says Tom. "Ah, yes…"

*   *   *

"What you up to Wednesday night?"

"Erm… going to a cookery class in solidarity with my flatmate. She's ashamed of her reliance on the microwave. Want to come?"

"No thanks. I already do a mean steak and chips. May I demonstrate on… Thursday, perhaps?"

During Ryan's pause, he mentally ensures that his parents will be out. His father would almost certainly give the game away, and his mother is, frankly, insufferable. Nobody deserves to be subjected to her tireless monologue: "Do you want a cup of tea? Do you want an apple? Do you two want to share this packet of Cheetos? I don't like them. Not sure why I bought them…"

"Sure, sounds great! Where do you live?"

*   *   *

"You're going to his house?" Jacek asks disapprovingly, five minutes later. He had heard the conversation from the other side of the canteen.

"Yes. Why? Don't you like him?"

"Has he said anything to offend you yet?" asks Jacek in response.

"No. What sort of thing?"

"You'll find out."

"Jacek!"

"Really, I don't like to say. It was disgusting."

"Well, if he says anything bad, I'll tell him off," says Lily mildly.

She knows that not everyone is as accepting, or as educated, as her, and that many people at Hope's repeat the *Daily Mail*'s views verbatim. She only tells them off if it's worth it, and since Ryan is only nineteen and says he doesn't like politics, she's sure she can gently bring him round to a broader understanding of the world.

"Do you like him?" asks Jacek.

"So far, yes. He's very open and approachable, not to mention cute."

"Am I cute?"

"No, you're hot, and so's your girlfriend. How are things?"

"Same old, same old," says Jacek, smiling somewhat ruefully as he departs in the direction of the shop floor.

He is not quite telling the truth. After the revival phase of their relationship, following the Lily incident, things have become somewhat stagnant between Jacek and Gabriela.

"You know, I would like to do what Lily did," says Gabriela to Jacek that evening. "Travel around Europe."

"Sounds like fun. When do you want to go?"

Gabriela hesitates. "Actually, is it okay if I plan to go with my girlfriends, rather than with you?"

"Of course. If I get this job, I'll have to work hard at it for a while, anyway."

Gabriela looks somewhat diminished. "You won't miss me?"

He walks over and hugs her. "Of course I'll miss you, baby, but you won't be gone forever, and you're twenty. You should be doing different things while you're young."

She smiles sweetly at him, and then goes to check her Facebook. Unbeknown to Jacek, she is having an early-twenties crisis. *I met my perfect man when I was eighteen,* she thinks; *therefore, I am set for early motherhood.* She's surprised by how much this thought scares her. Previously, she had assumed that as soon as she met the man of her dreams, she would want to settle down. Now, she sees all her friends doing different, exciting things – Lily just back from travelling, Agnieszka opening her own fashion boutique aged just twenty three, Maryja about to go on holiday to Barbados with her exciting older boyfriend, Marek winning his first sailing title. What is Gabriela doing? Working in a bookmaker's and a supermarket, living with the man she loves but is starting to feel detached from, doing a bit of partying and a bit of watching telly. She could have done that in Poland. She will still be able to do it when she is forty five. Why is she doing it here and now?

Jacek, for his part, still loves Gabriela, increasingly so since she stopped organising his life for him. He is simply concerned about her emotional responses. She seems not to know what she wants; smothering, jealous love, or a little independence. Jacek is confused by confusion. He is a generally straightforward person. When faced with another person's emotional turmoil, he is open, caring and supportive, but that doesn't mean he has any answers. As we have seen, when faced with his own dilemmas, his decisions are terrible.

* * *

"Mm-mm," says Lily appreciatively. "I must say, having burned the chow mein in yesterday's class, that you're talented, and this is a real treat."

She is munching her way through a medium-well done steak and a plate of crunchy chips. Ryan has excelled himself.

"Glad to be of service," he says, twinkling his blue eyes across the table at Lily. "'Fraid there's no dessert, though. That's Mum's forte, and she's at a school governor's meeting."

"How about a pint, a bag of crisps and a Europa league qualifier instead?"

"What an excellent idea. Beats raspberry trifle any day."

They end up in an old man's pub, where Ryan is known and liked. The TV screen is small, but there's hardly anybody watching it. Ryan certainly isn't. He's finding watching Lily drink a pint of Gale's HSB far more entertaining than the football.

"I can't believe you like real ale! What kind of hot girl are you?"

"One who's mother is an evangelist for Jesus and real ale."

"Your mum?"

"Yes. Dad's Irish, so Guinness is more his thing. Mum's got seven brothers, so she has some manly habits."

"So, was she a keep-trying-until-you-hit-the-jackpot baby?"

"What?" Lily hasn't heard that one before.

"I mean, did they want a girl really badly?"

"Oh, no – she was meant to be the third of four, but the fourth turned out to be triplets, and the twins were a surprise."

"How did they cope financially?" Ryan's temporarily forgotten all the nonsense he talked with his friends the other night, and is genuinely enjoying the conversation.

"Granny got a job. House prices were sane back then, so two incomes was usually enough if one of them was a good job, and my granddad was an architect."

"Did he design anything good?"

"Mostly people's houses, on the Isle of Wight," explains Lily. "He helped put a really old church back together after half of it fell down in that big storm of 1987. That made the local paper, and he retired that year, so he was pleased to have done something really worthwhile before he quit."

"He's still alive?"

"Yes – eighty four. His dad got a telegram from the Queen, so I expect we'll have him for a while yet. Do you have grandparents?"

"Only two. That's why I don't smoke."

"Oh, sorry," says Lily, looking humbly down at her pint.

"No apology necessary. You wouldn't have stopped my granddad from smoking if you wallpapered his bedroom with pictures of his cancerous lung. He believed in live fast, die young, but he never seemed as happy as my granddad who's alive. He never stopped complaining about stuff… Neither does my dad, really."

Lily isn't really watching the football either now. She and Ryan share their secrets until the landlord attempts to take their pints away with mock force.

"If you don't leave, Ryan, I'll suddenly remember that when Bridget ID'd you last week, I found out that you'd been tricking me for two years before your eighteenth."

Ryan chuckles, his cheeky grin and shining eyes lighting up his face. He walks Lily home, and they kiss on her doorstep.

21

"Tonia, will you look at this!"

"What is it?" Tonia wanders from the TV to where Lily is looking at the computer screen.

"Football Supporters' Europe wants a researcher for their office in Hamburg! They say you need intermediate German, but fluent English. Most of the work they do is bilingual. I've got A Level German, and I'd love to work abroad."

"Go for it!" says Tonia immediately, then, thoughtfully, "Do you think Ryan would want to live in Germany?"

"No idea, but anyway, I probably won't even get an interview. Why would they want me, when a hundred thousand fanzine editors are applying for the job as we speak?"

"Didn't you write for the university sports paper?"

"In second year, yes, when I thought I might want to be a journalist one day. A language-based degree is a plus, too, as they want the researcher to write press releases and emails. They'll know that someone with a degree in English Lit isn't illiterate."

"Well, as I said, go for it. We both believe that God's will will be done if we ask for it."

* * *

"But Lily, I *want* to see you naked."

"I know, and believe me, I'm not saying no for lack of attraction. It's just… I've been such a slut all my life, and now I want to change. Do you understand?"

"So, you're not a virgin?"

Lily and Ryan have been kissing on his sofa, on another parents-free evening, and are discussing whether or not to go to his bedroom and take things further.

"I'm not, but I've only slept with one man. I've… done too much stuff with too many men. I want to behave myself from now on, until…"

"You get married?"

"Yes."

Ryan frowns. "Actually," he says, truthfully, "I've always believed in traditional relationships, but been a hypocrite, because I like sex. No, scratch that – I love sex. So maybe I could practice not having sex with you. If it works out between us, I'll get my reward in full one day. If not, I'll find out whether I'm able to do what I think is right."

As Lily kisses Ryan goodbye at the door, he starts to think he might not be able to go through with the plan to mess her about. Then reality kicks in, and he thinks, *Nah, she's a socialist. Screw her... or not, as the case may be.*

When Lily gets home, there is a phone message from Coral. "Lils, why aren't you answering your mobile? I'm going to publish my cookbook!"

Coral didn't manage to get her cookbook endorsed by UEFA, but cracked on nonetheless, removing any content that might belong to another copyright holder.

"Call me when you get this, even if it's the middle of the night. Bye!"

Tonia is already in bed, so Lily calls back straightaway, instead of going to tell her flatmate the news.

"Coral – it's like nearly the end of August. How are you going to publish it? And what do you mean, 'you'?"

"I couldn't get a publisher to commit, but one of them said they would print it if I paid for the first 1000 copies, then see how they sold. I said I didn't have that kind of money, but when I told my mum, she got all emotional and said my granny would have wanted me to be successful, and therefore I could use some of the money she left us. So it's going to be available on Amazon – and in Brent Cross' Waterstones, 'cos they like to support local authors – from next Friday, 'cos that's when the draw is!"

"Wow! So are you launching it at Brent Cross?"

"Sadly not, 'cos somebody people have heard of is doing a reading there on Friday afternoon, but I'm organising a launch in the local church hall, where my granny served sausage rolls at kids' parties for forty years."

"Put me down for a copy, Coral. I can't wait! And I'll help you publicise the launch. I love doing things like that."

Lily hangs up, filled with vicarious happiness. A new boyfriend, and good news for her friend's career. Will good things come in threes?

The day of the launch comes around quickly. Lily wakes up, prays, puts her uniform on, and goes to check her email.

"Tonia, I've got an interview!"

"Where?" Tonia comes to look over Lily's shoulder, trying not to cover her friend in juice from her grapefruit portion.

"Here. The telephone. Wednesday at three."

"For which job?"

"You know. THAT job!"

"Oh, wow!" squeals Tonia. "I guess Hamburg is a bit far to make you travel for an interview. Well done for getting one. What did you tell them?"

"The truth, and I didn't send a photograph!"

Tonia had insisted that the male-dominated nature of such an organisation would make this a good idea, but Lily refused to capitulate to sexism.

"Well, good luck. Imagine you living in Germany!"

* * *

"Are you seeing Ryan?"

"Yes, how did you know?"

Lily has a shift before it is time to get on the train to London, and is being interrogated by Jacek about her love life.

"I saw you on Portswood Road. You looked cute and cuddly."

"You look upset."

"I don't like him," says Jacek flatly.

Jacek thinks about whether or not to tell her the gory details. "Have you asked him his political views?"

"He's not into politics. His eyes glaze over when I talk about it. What has he said?"

"Stuff that would make you angry."

Jacek doesn't like the idea of telling on Ryan – neither of them are primary school children – but doesn't like the thought of Lily getting disappointed in love again, either.

"Well, if he says anything, I'll tell him why he's wrong, and if he's a decent person, he'll be open to new ideas. I'm not inclined to turn him into me," says Lily firmly. "Yes, I have strong views, but as long as someone's not a Nazi fascist, I think I could live with them."

"Okay." Jacek grabs Lily's shoulders as she turns to leave, and looks deep into her eyes. "Don't get hurt, Lily."

"Jacek, honey… I won't do anything reckless. In fact, I'm treading more carefully than ever before. But I can't spend the rest of my life being too careful, trying not to get hurt… Oh, I forgot to tell you." Thinking about the rest of her life has reminded her. "I got an interview for that football job in Hamburg!"

"What? You have to go to Germany for an interview?"

"No, it's over the phone, but I'll have to move there if I get it!"

"I'll miss you."

"Same." She smiles, somewhat ruefully. "Anyway, we're assuming I'll get the job. I expect the competition will be amazing."

Jacek puts his arm around Lily. "You are amazing, therefore they will want you, and I will have to miss you." He finally manages to make his way downstairs after that.

The launch is an incredible success. Lily and Coral have worked together to compile an impressive guest list. It turns out that the local MP used to be a food writer for the *Sunday Express*, and seems genuinely interested in the book, and delighted to attend the launch. The Vice Chancellor of Middlesex University turns up because Coral's sister Elaine did her photography degree there, and all Coral's old school friends have turned out for the occasion. Lily, Heidi, Tonia and Coral are reunited for the first time since the holiday. Simon and Ryan declined to come.

"Simon thinks cooking is a waste of time, and in any case, he's got band practice," says Tonia apologetically.

"Ryan had no money for the coach," adds Lily. "I don't think he would have enjoyed this, though. I can't imagine him sipping wine and asking erudite questions about food writing. He actually asked if I didn't think it was a bit 'modern football'."

"And what do you think?" asks Coral.

"I think it's only realistic to assume that today's ticket prices confine many people to watching football on television. I also think this book could be a great school resource – encouraging young boys to cook. I like the practical nature of what you've done, Coral. Anyone with half an hour to spare can make these recipes, meaning they're not a distraction from going to football, or a middle-class indulgence."

"Me, too," says Tonia. "I've no idea what any of that means, but they sound like cool things to think."

"She means a pie-muncher like me could knock any of these up after a day down the pits," says Heidi, to general amusement.

In the end, Coral sells one hundred and fifty books on the night, with plenty of promises to buy online. Things are looking great.

"So, you're really going to move to Germany?" Heidi asks Lily.

"Maybe… Well, definitely if I get offered the job, and probably not if I don't."

"Will Ryan go with you?"

"We'll cross that bridge when we come to it. I've known him for all of three weeks. I assume not, at first. If we're getting on really well by the time I have to go, being separated will be a good test of how much we want to be together. How's it going with Benito, Heidi?"

"Well, it's hard to tell from phone calls and emails, but underneath the unbelievable good looks, he's actually a charming person who seems interested in my life, so… we'll see. As soon as I get some holiday, I'll visit him, and we'll see if the magic's still there"

"So six different men might never see you naked?"

"Doubt it, Lily. You might be behaving yourself for the time being, but you'll always be the sluttiest of them all!" smiles Heidi smugly. She means no offence, and none is taken.

*   *   *

As far as Lily is aware, her interview goes well. The next day, Jacek announces that he is to be the new grocery manager. He is clearly very proud and happy. Lily can't help but hug him.

"You'll be amazing. You're so good with people, and so organised."

"You would not say that if you could see my bedroom," growls Jacek, before realising what he's said and blushing crimson.

A few people heard, too, judging by the assorted, "Ooooh!" noises.

"I bet Gabriela's so proud of you, in spite of the problems in the bedroom," Lily jokes.

She's called away by Frank then, and doesn't see Jacek wince. Things have not been wonderful in the bedroom for a week or two now, and he is starting to wonder if he should be worried. Case in point – the previous evening.

"Jacek! I'm not in the mood!"

All he had done was start to knead the knots from Gabriela's shoulders while she sat at the computer. He hadn't been trying to initiate sex.

"I'm doing this because I love you, and you looked so worried."

"I'm fine," she had said, abruptly.

"Okay." Jacek had smoothed the heels of his hands across her shoulders, and then released her.

Gabriela liked this motion, and started to wonder if she had been a little hasty.

"Okay, Jacek, if you insist," she had said, then turned, and started to unbutton his shirt…

Jacek smiled, and kissed her forehead. "If *you* insist. I was just being nice…"

They'd made love then, but Gabriela had seemed a little unresponsive. Jacek couldn't help but think back to the days when lovemaking had been her favourite activity. Now, he snuggled into her, and kissed her.

"How do you feel?"

She squirmed a little. "Not so sleepy as usual. I think I'll start dinner."

Jacek had watched her go with a nagging sensation at the back of his mind. He couldn't shake the feeling that this was not a good sign.

* * *

"So she won't even shag you? Ryan, you poor sap. You should get out of there," says Ian.

"Yeah, but then we won't get to have any fun," argues Tom. "What are we going to do, anyway?" The boys confer over their pints, finally deciding upon a good strategy.

"It'll be a walk in the park," cracks Marcus, and everyone laughs.

* * *

"Ryan, would you want to try and make our relationship work if I moved abroad?"

"You're serious about going to Germany?"

"It would be an amazing opportunity, and I think it would be good to do it before I've got… kids and stuff."

Ryan notices the pause. "Do you think you'll want kids?"

"Yes. Do you?"

"Yes, but you seemed to find it hard to say."

"I was pregnant earlier this year," explains Lily heavily, knowing that this conversation has to take place sooner or later. "I lost it."

"Ouch." Once again, Ryan feels for Lily, but not enough to stop plotting against her. He is developing two fairly distinct personalities, and is in severe danger of ending up in hospital, although he doesn't realise it. "So, you and your one shag were pretty serious, then?"

Lily hesitates. "Yes and no. I was in love with him, but we didn't last long. He was still in love with his ex."

"And are they together still?"

"Yes."

Ryan sighs deeply. "And are you still in love with him?"

Lily has to think hard. "Not so much that I'm emotionally unavailable, but I think I'll always like him, fancy him and be passionate about him, even if I fall in love, marry and have kids with someone else."

Ryan shakes his head. "I don't know how you girls do it. How can you feel all that stuff for one person and still have a boyfriend?" *The same way you can be so nice to this girl when you secretly want to kick her head in*, says the voice of reason, which he ignores. Listening to it makes him feel uncomfortable.

"Because it's necessary to try and move on – and quite enjoyable, too, and you're the only one who gets to feel this." She kisses him.

22

After a few weeks, Lily comes to realise that she might actually love Ryan. On the day of their sixth date, a scouting trip to watch Eastleigh- a local non-League side- play football against Ryan's team's next opponents, she realises she has butterflies at the thought of having him all to herself for a few hours, rather than having to share him at work. She is thinking about this when the phone rings, catapulting her out of her reverie.

"Hello. Can I speak to Lily McGoldrick, please?" The caller is a central European-accented woman.

"Speaking."

"My name is Gretel, from the FSE. I will get straight to the point. We've decided to offer you the job of Research Assistant."

"Why, thank you!" Lily takes a deep breath, says a silent prayer, and her next words are, "I accept your offer. When do I start?"

A few miles away, another person is thinking about Europe.

"Jacek, I think I might want to start travelling in January," says Gabriela, hovering in the doorway of the living room.

"Fine by me. How long for?"

"I don't know. I have started saving money, but it will depend on how much I can save in three months."

Jacek walks over and kisses her. "Take all the time you need. You are still young. I don't want to chain you to the cooker and the sink."

Gabriela has become increasingly distant over these intervening weeks, and Jacek is doing his best to be normal-but-nice. He doesn't want to push her away with emotional suffocation, but he does want to make an effort to reinvigorate their relationship. Little does he know that Gabriela is suffering from a distraction he knows only two well…

Three Weeks Earlier

A rap on her window at Ladbrokes, and Gabriela looks up to see a man two or three years older than her. He has brown hair and eyes, and a smattering of freckles, but the most striking thing about his appearance is that he has chosen to wear a shiny purple shirt.

"Sorry to disturb you. It's my first day today. I have to see Mr. Swift."

"Okay, come to the white door on the left. I will let you in."

Mr Swift turns out to be in a meeting, and Gabriela and this young man, whose name is Jamie, are able to converse for longer.

"I've just finished my degree," he tells her. "I haven't managed to get a job, and I need some money. I might do teacher training next year, if I don't find anything."

"Oh, my friend Lily has the same problem. She works at Hope's – that's where my other job is. What did you do at university?"

"History, at Aston University. So you're a hard-working Pole with two jobs?"

"I think I am more of a money-spending Pole."

They both laugh. The next day, Jamie arrives at ten again, and is working next to Gabriela all day.

"Gabi, someone's given me a fifty-pound note. What do I do?"

She shows him the secure clip under the desk. For a brief second, their hands touch as they both try to insert the note, and Gabriela feels a spark of electricity that she knows she ought not to feel…

Two weeks later, Jamie and Gabriela are best buddies. She knows all about his split from his last girlfriend, who he describes as 'like a machine… A housekeeping robot, with no lust for life whatsoever." She felt a twinge of guilt when he told her this, and a realisation that if Jacek hadn't had a mid-relationship crisis, she could have ended up the same way. Jamie knows all about her travel plans, and that she lives with a boyfriend and seems content. He is a good boy, and would not dream of upsetting Gabriela's applecart… Well, he would not do it, although he certainly dreams about taking Jacek's place. Gabriela is the stuff that dreams are made of, after all.

They are talking about Gabriela's travel plans.

"So, your boyfriend won't go with you?"

"No. He has a new job. It is too complicated. Anyway, I think I want to do this with women only." She smiles. "I have lived with a man for too long."

Jamie frowns, and turns back to his work.

"What?" asks Gabriela.

"Just that if it was me, I think I would want my girlfriend to come, terribly badly. It's not like it's a weekend away, is it? I'd miss her. I suppose he could come out for a holiday and see you, couldn't he?"

"I suppose."

Does she really want Jacek to come and see her? She goes to the water cooler. As she is pouring her drink, she realises she would *love* Jamie to come and visit her on her travels, and the thought shakes her rigid. What does it *mean*?

That evening is the evening when Jacek and Gabriela sleep together, but she scurries away immediately afterwards. He was right; she did not enjoy it as much as usual. What, she thinks, is wrong with me, so that my perfect man can't send me into raptures anymore?

Or is he someone else's perfect man – someone sparky, lively, untidy and adventurous – and is mine a cuddly, well-dressed home bird whose ex-girlfriend was my ex-self?

* * *

Lily goes to work on a high.

"Jacek," she squeals as soon as she sees him, "I got the job."

He squeezes her arm. "That's fantastic! When do you start?"

"They've given me four weeks. I'll leave here in three. My first day will be the nineteenth of October."

He looks into her eyes, as has become his custom when he has something serious to say.

"We must keep in touch. Do you promise?"

"Of course. If Gabriela's going to travel around Europe, you could come and visit us both. She'll keep us out of trouble."

He smiles, nods, and then sighs. "Lily, I do not usually say things like this, but whether I marry Gabriela and you marry stupid Ryan or not, we have been through too much together for you ever to be not in my life. Do you agree?"

His faltering grammar makes the sentiment melt Lily's heart even more than one would expect.

"Yes. Maybe our kids will be together. I'd like a Bogdanowski in the family, by hook or by crook."

"Be careful, Lily. We are trouble!"

She doesn't care. She doesn't care about work. She doesn't care about time and space. She doesn't care about… No, wait, she does…

* * *

"Is it possible to love two people at the same time?"

Tonia raises her head from the newspaper in mild exasperation. "Jacek?"

"Of course. You won't believe what he said to me today."

After hearing Lily's story, Tonia is more sympathetic.

"That's cute. He's nicer than when you first told me about him, by the sound of things."

"Yes – he's changed a bit. He's being nicer to everybody, but still *totally* not boring," sighs Lily. "Literally perfect. But not for me, and I do like Ryan – maybe even love him. I just wish Jacek would stop being Jacek for long enough for me to stop comparing Ryan with him."

"You're moving to Germany," says Tonia gently. "That will make or break you and Ryan, and put distance between you and Jacek. You'll who what you feel. Perhaps the person you're destined to be with is really Hans or Fritz."

"Well, never mind Hans and Fritz right now – there's Ryan to think about. See you this evening, if you're still awake!"

Lily grabs her bag and runs out of the door to the bus stop.

*   *   *

"DON'T MOVE!" Hand over the money! All of it! NOW!"

"We cannot open the tills unless a transaction is being made." Gabriela's voice is shaking in terror.

"Give us the f***ing money, Polak! We'll put a tenner on the 3.30 at Kempton if we have to!"

The three masked, black-clad men have pistols, and all the staff are petrified beyond words. Jamie nods, enters a fake transaction, and opens his till, praying for the arrival of the police.

"What's going on? Oh, no!" Mr Swift has emerged from his office.

One of the robbers waves his pistol energetically. "You! Open the safe! NOW!"

"Certainly not. I shall call the police." Mr Swift knows the glass between the robbers and him is bullet-proof. The robber does, too, and he fires a shot at it to speed up proceedings.

Jamie takes no risks. He flings Gabriela's chair over, pushing her to the floor and out of the way of the bullet. There is a loud crack as the glass shatters, but does not break.

Mercifully, a fire alarm installation engineer has had a mild heart attack two streets away. His life is in no immediate danger. The robbers mistake the ambulance sirens for police sirens, swear, and leave without any money.

Gabriela gets up off the floor, looks straight at Jamie, bursts into tears, and says the only English words she can manage right now: "Thank you." She goes to give him a friendly hug and kiss on the cheek, but in her tender emotional state, she is drawn to kiss him properly, and cannot fight her desire.

*   *   *

Jacek comes home from work, turns the TV on, and slumps down on the sofa.
"Gabi?" No response. He calls her mobile; it rings out. He closes his eyes…

The front door opens half an hour later, waking Jacek.

"Gabi, where have you been?"

"The police station," she says, in a small voice. "We were robbed… Well, they tried. They fired a shot."

Jacek swears and runs over to her. "My poor baby. Did it hit the glass?"

"Yes. It will have to be replaced. Jacek, I have something to tell you." She takes a deep breath. "Jamie pushed me out of the way of the bullet. I was so scared that I forgot the glass. I forgot everything. I thought I was going to die. When I didn't die…" She starts to cry. "I kissed Jamie. At first I thought I wasn't thinking straight, and had been stupid. But… I have been thinking. We were waiting so long at the station, and I was on my own." A shudder runs through Gabriela, as she psyches herself up to speak the unspeakable. "Jacek, I want to be single for a while. I don't think I love you anymore. I think I love Jamie, but to find out, I need to be on my own. I am so, so sorry. None of this is your fault."

Even though things have been a bit odd for a while, Jacek still feels shocked by the suddenness of this announcement. He is silent for a time, and then manages to say what he always knew he would say, if this ever happened.

"Go. I forgive you absolutely. You must do what you have to do. Where will you stay?"

"With Elzbieta, for a while. Her flatmate moved back to Gdansk, and she needs help with the rent. It will be cheaper than here." She smiles, a tiny smile. "Thank you for being so good."

"Can I kiss you goodbye?"

She nods, and they share a final, tearful, warm moment of a comfortable, warm relationship. Jacek's heart is pounding and aching, but not breaking. Having nearly lost his love to death, losing her to the free life of a single young woman doesn't seem apocalyptic, somehow.

*   *   *

Lily and Ryan walk, arm in arm, from the central station to the main street of Southampton, Above Bar Street. Lily expects them to turn right, but instead Ryan says, "Let's go to the Angel of the South," and crosses over into the park.

"So, did you enjoy the game?" he asks.

"It wasn't bad, for a 0-0. Do you think your team'll beat them?"

"It'll be another 0-0, unless that left-back breaks his leg. He cuts out everything down that wing, and that's where we're dangerous, but their strikers are useless,"

"Did you ever get a trial, or anything?" asks Lily, knowing that Ryan plays on that dangerous right wing.

"Yeah, Chelsea. They said I was too small, yet still signed Shaun Wright-Phillips."

"And left him on the bench for three years. Some bad decisions can seem so right at the time."

"Like going out with me, you mean?"

Lily takes Ryan's hand. "Nope. That was an excellent decision. Whether it'll end in marriage and babies or not, I still think seeing you is a fantastic use of my time."

"Even though you're a university graduate and I'm thick as a plank?"

"When you learn about politics, you'll learn that the socialist attitude to education is not one of intellectual snobbery. In English, that means I like you – maybe, I'm not a hundred percent sure but maybe, even love you – for who you are." She takes a deep breath. Has she said too much?

Ryan's heart is pounding, his hands starting to sweat. He can't go through with his plan now. He genuinely likes Lily McGoldrick. Not agreeing with her doesn't mean he has to hurt her – and her soft-yet-incisive words are making his points of disagreement with her disappear. He steers her to the left. "Let's go this way."

"Are you sure? I think the pub's straight on."

"Yeah. We're taking the Polish alcoholic-free route," Ryan improvises rapidly. "I could see a big gang of them. I don't want you being harassed by angry Poles."

"The story of my life."

A few metres away, Ryan's three friends see the pair change direction.

"The ponce," curses Tom. "Has he chickened out?"

"Bollocks to that. No money from all our hard work earlier on, now no reward at the end of a hard day – not having it! Let's go!"

"Lily," Ryan is saying, "thank you for saying you might love me. I need to think hard before I can ever say anything like that to you, but it's appealing to know that I'm dating an honest woman."

"You might make an honest woman of me one day," Lily teases.

Thud.

A big stone has hit her on the ankle. She turns to see three lads, dressed in black, leering at her.

"Oi," she yells, "watch it, will you?"

Ryan swears internally. "Walk faster, Lily."

Smack. One hits her on the back of the hand. She starts to run, but the boys are faster. One rugby tackles her around the waist. Another yanks her head back harshly by her hair.

"HELP! STOP!" she screams.

"Please, please, stop, you wankers," Ryan begs as Marcus kicks Lily in the stomach. "It's off."

What's off? Lily thinks.

"F**k that, Ryan, we've been looking forward to this for weeks," Ian shouts.

"Ryan, do you *know* these people? AAAAAAAAAAH!" The boots and fists are relentless. "RYAN! DO SOMETHING!"

"Come on, boys, time to go." The lads become tired of their new game and scarper, leaving Ryan on his hands and knees beside Lily, whispering, "I'm sorry, babe. I'm so, so sorry."

"Who were they?" Lily gasps, struggling to breathe, unable to stand.

"National Front."

"How do you know them?" Ryan's silence speaks for itself.

"I'll call an ambulance, Lily, I'm so sorry." He runs away.

* * * *

Jacek has just helped Gabriela load the last of her boxes in Elzbieta's car. "Call me when you get there," he says. One last kiss on the cheek, the revving of an engine, and she is gone.

He needs to clear his head. He turns, and begins to pound up Bevois Valley Road. What would make him feel better? A drink? No, he doesn't feel like it. A fag? Definitely. He lights one, continuing to walk. A little better, but not much. His loss is a sore ulcer, in the part of the body that feels warm in Lily when she is in love, somewhere above the stomach. Maybe he'll go clubbing – some music to drown out the pain. He heads for town. He stops in the Polish shop on Charlotte Place roundabout for more cigarettes, and a comforting chat in his native language. He feels a little lighter. He crosses the road and walks into the park.

At a crossroads of the many paths in the park, he hears a pathetic sound, like a hurt dog. He sees a dark shape on the ground. He turns at once to investigate. Somebody, or something, is suffering worse than he. The thing emits a tiny word. 'Help.' It is a woman, not a dog. Who could have done this to a woman? Who could have done this to…

"Lily!" He pulls her into a sitting position, his heart breaking at last. She is bleeding from her nose, mouth, and stomach. One eye is black, and she can barely keep either open.

"Jacek, help me. Am I dead?"

"No, babe, you're going to be fine." He pulls his phone out to call an ambulance, only to see one arrive, flanked by a police car. "We have to stop meeting like this, though," Jacek sighs. He brushes her hair out of her face, and kisses a pure spot on her battered cheek. He feels better, and awful, at the same time.

"Why did you think you were dead?" he asks her in the ambulance.

"Because you'll be waiting when I get to Heaven."

"What? Who says I'll die first?"

"That's just how it works. You might not have died first – time won't matter. Anyway, you're older, and I'm a woman, and I don't smoke. Mind you, I'm very accident-prone."

Some oxygen has perked Lily up. A middle-aged woman approaches her stretcher bed.

"Hi, Lily. My name is Sylvia Carr. I'm a police officer. We need to ask you some questions about the incident. Did you know your attackers?"

"Friends of my boyfriend's. I'd never met them before." She winces as a paramedic shifts slightly while holding a cloth against the wound on her stomach. "I think he set me up."

"WHAT?" Jacek gets to his feet, as if expecting to see Ryan come into the ambulance to receive a punch in the face.

"Relax, please, sir. We'll handle this. Had you had an argument?"

"No. I think he was stringing me along. He didn't tell me he was in the National Front, and I told him I'm a socialist."

Jacek can't take any more. He wants to get off today's emotional rollercoaster.

"Lily, that thing he said – it was something racist about Frank and Lynn. I should have told you. I didn't think it would turn out to be serious information. I mean, I thought you could change anyone…"

"Don't let me change you, Jacek. I like you just the way you are. And don't worry. You were right – if he was being honest, and didn't like politics, but had some bigoted views, he probably would have changed as he grew up."

"But you *have* changed me. I have stopped being mean to people because I think they look unhealthy, or lazy. I have seen how much you eat, and are still like this." Jacek draws an hourglass with his hands. "I can see that there is some luck involved here."

"Sorry, Lily, but I have a few more questions for you," interjects Sylvia, who is still in the ambulance, being unintentionally ignored.

As Sylvia grills her, pieces start to fall into place in Jacek's philosophical jigsaw puzzle. He thinks about passion, and change. An ideal partner should inspire one to virtual worship, and equally inspire one to change for the better. Will he ever again find a woman who is carved in stone with him in mind? Suddenly, and without the possibility of regret, he knows what he must do.

Wednesday isn't too bad a night for drunks, and Lily gets patched up fairly quickly. She pays for hire of a crutch to support her sprained ankle for a few days, and Jacek ushers her out into the night.

"Gabriela was also a victim of crime today," he says matter-of-factly.

"Really? What happened?"

"She was shot at."

"Oh my word! Is she OK?"

"Yes. It made her think. She has decided to be on her own for a while."

"Is that a good idea? If it was me, I'd want lots of hugs that night…"

"She is having hugs from her friend Elzbieta. She is taking a break from relationships."

"What?" gasps Lily. "But if something like that happened to me, I'd just want to fall into your arms."

Oh dear – it looks like Lily has said what she is thinking again, and it is not always wise to do so.

"So, why don't you?"

Jacek opens his arms wide to welcome the woman who was created with his happiness in mind, and Lily, filled with a sudden, urgent joy, kisses the last person she will ever see naked as if her life depends on it. Behind them, ambulances and taxis arrive and leave, people nurse broken arms into A and E, and psychiatrists smoke their accursed cigarettes. Above them, heavenly choirs sing, God observes the working out of his master plan in spite of the usual human attempts to derail it, and, in Lily's overactive imagination, tickertape falls over her and Jacek. The world has stopped to enjoy their beautiful moment.

Epilogue

Hi, I'm Kate Bogdanowski-Baker.

I used to be Kasia at primary school, but then I got sick of being called Casio Calculator, and I *am* half English, so I went for Kate from year seven onwards. My brother Wojciech doesn't have such an easy option.

Anyway, Mum did go to Germany, and Dad stayed behind, but for the four weeks before she left, she enjoyed the I'm-kissing-Jacek feeling, the incredulous and fabulous joy, every time an opportunity arose to kiss him. She lived in Hamburg for a year, and Dad visited her every month, and she revelled in telling her new friends all about her boyfriend, feeling her heart leap and scream 'I'm Jacek's girlfriend!' every time she did. On her last night – coincidentally, her last day as a twenty two-year-old – Dad took Mum into the St Pauli stadium while it was closed, and proposed in the centre circle. It was partly Amos' idea. He, Mum and Dad are still friends to this day.

Gabriela is a good family friend. She went out with Jamie for a year, but he turned out to be too dull for her. It was her lack of stimuli that was responsible for her lack of personality. Travelling changed everything, and now she even makes the odd joke! Would you believe she's married to Benito? Heidi brought him to Coral's next book launch, but as a friend. They'd grown tired of each other, and tired of the distance. Mum and Dad brought Gabriela because she'd just split up with Jamie and was bored and lonely, and the rest is history.

Coral has written six books about recipes, and two about the history of publishing, which ended up being her specialist subject when she went on Mastermind. She didn't do very well on general knowledge, though. It didn't help that she answered a question about who won the treble in 1999 with 'Manc scum… Oh, sorry, I mean Manchester United.' Sadly, John Humphries had to take her first answer.

Coral took a while to find the right man, but had fun trying. She spent two years in the south of France, writing a book about rural French cuisine, and having a wonderfully torrid affair with a local goatherd who looked uncannily like Robert Pires. Unfortunately, a Parisian model agency came calling, and the goatherd decided that his new lifestyle meant a new girlfriend, who didn't cook, and only ate tissues and lettuce. Returning to England in some distress, Coral had a crying fit on Platform 4 at Southampton Central station, and a man six years her junior asked her if she was okay. Martin Mullins and his stepmum Sally, formerly Hill, took her to the Station Hotel for an emergency alcoholic beverage, and the rest, as they say, is history. Sally, incidentally, met her dream man, Craig Mullins, on her first day at her dream job. She got her miracle, and has never had to use Botox.

Heidi is living in sin with a Welsh rugby player called Darren Bellamy. They have spawned two twenty-something rugby players. They keep talking about marriage, but at the end of the day, Heidi can't be arsed to have to eat poncey food and pretend to be nice to her mother-in-law while wearing a white dress, not even for a few hours.

Tonia is having a great time too, with Simon, of course. For one who used to hate thinking, she's become rather full of philosophical insight. She managed to reconcile her family just before her wedding, and her mum has mellowed in her old age, becoming something of an ambassador for Christian unity in spite of theological differences.

My mum became Mrs Lily Bogdanowski on the 13th of April 2014, and walked around in a delighted haze for months, mithering about being married to Jacek – Dad, I mean – to anyone who would listen, including Dad, who was slightly embarrassed, but secretly thrilled by the constant ego massage. After leaving the FSE, she moved back to England and formed an organisation dedicated to reintroducing atmosphere at English football grounds. She financed herself through freelance sports writing, using her degree after all. After getting married, she and Dad decamped to Poland for a while because my great-grandmother was dying, and I was born in

Lodz, but raised in Southampton. By the time Dad retired, he was a supermarket general manager. He was never as ambitious as Mum; he wanted a job that he could forget about at the end of the day. He still did very well for himself, and when I was a child, I noticed that the colleagues who told me what a great manager he was seemed to have honest faces.

Mum still works, currently for the National Union of Students, managing various student welfare schemes. I think most days she'd rather be a student, standing on the correct side of the mental health table and looking after people directly. She still does football activism on the side. Flares are allowed at all football grounds in the EU now, essentially because of my mum. She's still more proud of being Mrs Jacek Bogdanowski than of anything she's achieved, and now that she's filled in the back story, I know why.

In spite of her successful career, my mum was more than happy to take a break and have children as a relatively young woman. I waited longer, but when I was thirty and brought my twin daughters into the world, I began to understand my mother's indulgent smile – the daft look that crossed her features when my brother and I did apparently mundane things. You can't understand that without becoming a mother. I think most children spend most of their childhood thinking their parents have either gone soft in the head, or don't respect them. The laughter when you use a big word and you're only five? I used to find that highly insulting, but I inflicted that on my daughters and son, too. It's a parent's prerogative to be sweetly annoying, knowing that as long as they procreate, our offspring will understand one day.

Going further back, I've understood my mother's fanatical devotion to my father more since, aged twenty one, I found a boxed ring in my boyfriend's trouser pocket. I've loved Will from the moment I set eyes on him, but the thought of being Mrs Katarzyna Bogdanowski-Baker made my insides jump around and sing hymns, just like my mother's.

And I am just like my mother. Being alike isn't necessarily the key to getting along, and growing up I was a real Daddy's girl, but as I've got older, I've understood Mum more and more. I, too, am so addicted to solidarity… so happy to help, because it's just my job… so insanely in love.

Close your eyes, and picture something. Make it a shiny bright red sports car. Where does it live? I bet the picture is right before your eyes, like that line that tells you whether or not you're sitting in the right place for a passport photo. I bet the picture feels like it is deep inside your mind, maybe between your ears, directly below that spot at the top of your head that hurts when your neck's all tense. I also expect that the picture isn't very clear, and that you can barely make out the car's lines within the blackness of your mind – unless you're an artist, maybe. When I try to imagine the car, I guess I see what a literary person sees when she tries to imagine something.

Now, however, I see a girl in this part of my mind, clear as day, clear as if she had walked into my room. She looks twelve or thirteen years old. Her hair is the same colour as mine, blonde, but curly like Uncle Dan's, rather than straight like mine. She wears it longer than I would ever wear it, and doesn't care for it as well as I do mine – in a good way. You can tell she's never had a care in the world…

"Thank you for your story, Kate," says the Voice that told me to tell it. "Liljana liked it very much."